"**Y**ou can tell or ask me anything," Bruce said, looking at her and holding her gaze. "I promise I'll try to be as open and honest with you as possible."

Sage looked at him. He was so physically beautiful. It was impossible to look away from his piercing brown eyes. She couldn't tell or ask him anything; that would completely disrupt their working relationship.

Her heart did that little dip it usually did when they were in close proximity. "I er… I think…"

Bruce waited her out while she wet her lips nervously.

"You are never usually so reticent to articulate your thoughts."

"What were we talking about again?" Sage dragged her gaze away from his.

"You've been trying to break up with Brian."

"Yes," Sage nodded. "And it's frustrating. He won't listen. I'm just going to move on and let him get the message."

"Is there someone else?" Bruce asked, slowing to a crawl.

"I can't tell you," Sage said. "It's a secret. I just want to be free of Brian and move on."

"Oh," Bruce looked at her, then went silent.

"What are you thinking?" Sage asked.

"You don't want to know," Bruce said abruptly.

SAGE

BRENDA BARRETT

SAGE
A Jamaica Treasures Book/November2024
Published by Jamaica Treasures
Manchester, Jamaica

ISBN 978-976-97430-5-2

ALSO BY BRENDA BARRETT

FULL CIRCLE
NEW BEGINNINGS
THE PREACHER AND THE PROSTITUTE
AFTER THE END
THE EMPTY HAMMOCK
THE PULL OF FREEDOM
REBOUND SERIES
THREE RIVERS SERIES
NEW SONG SERIES
BANCROFT SERIES
MAGNOLIA SISTERS SERIES
SCARLETT SERIES
WILEY BROTHERS SERIES
PRYCE SISTERS SERIES
THE JACKSONS SERIES
CRIMSON HILL SERIES
SPICE AND STONE SERIES
RIDGEVIEW SERIES

ABOUT THE AUTHOR

Brenda Barrett is an award-winning and bestselling author who has a passion for writing real Jamaican romances.

When she's not weaving words that transport readers to exotic locales, you can find her nurturing her green thumb in the garden or doting on her beloved cats.

With an infectious zest for life, this author brings a unique perspective to her writing that is both relatable and thought-provoking.

Don't be surprised if you find yourself lost in the pages of her latest work, as she seamlessly blends romance with some drama, mystery, and suspense, or even sci-fi, leaving readers wanting more.

You can connect with Brenda online at:
Brenalbar.com
Twitter.com/AuthorWriterBB
Facebook.com/AuthorBrendaBarrett

Chapter One

"**S**age, can you come to my office, please?" Bruce Whitlock said briskly over the phone.

Sage jumped to attention guiltily. She had not been productive. Instead of working she was trading wedding dress ideas with her sister.

Cayenne and Dirk were having a wedding ceremony on the jetty at Sea Glass Villas, and the bride was conflicted about how sophisticated or simple her dress should be. It had turned into a family chat. Even her grandmother Rosemary was involved. They were all going to meet at a custom dress designer this evening at six. Sage liked a halter-neck, fishtail style that looked elegant and simple. She was so in love with the design that she pushed it on Cayenne like it was a life or death matter.

She only realized that she had accidentally grabbed the bridal magazine with her laptop when she was at the door to Bruce's office. She groaned inwardly. Brian proposed every other week these days, and she didn't want to give Bruce the impression that she had weddings on the brain or was thinking about marrying his son.

In fact, for the past six months, she had been trying to break up with Brian. It was just so hard to do with him away at school. He was doing his master's in engineering at Caltech, and he had returned home twice since then. Both times when she brought up the matter, he completely ignored her efforts to break up with him. He could be so frustrating.

She gritted her teeth. The last time he was here, three months ago, she had been as brutal as possible. "Brian, I simply don't love you. I don't think we are compatible."

His response had been to laugh as if she were joking. "Sage, you're just stressed. We've been together for so long; you probably can't imagine life without me. But trust me, it's just a phase. You'll see."

That dismissive attitude had left her seething for weeks. She had tried to give him space, hoping he'd realize the truth, but instead, he seemed more determined than ever to hold on to her. Sage was at her wit's end.

As she approached Bruce Whitlock's office, she took a deep breath and tried to compose herself. Bruce was not a man to be kept waiting, and she had already wasted enough time today. She knocked on the door, clutching her laptop and the bridal magazine.

"Come in," Bruce's voice boomed from inside.

Sage pushed the door open and stepped in, trying to hide the magazine under the laptop. Bruce looked better every time she saw him. He was the definition of tall, dark, and handsome. He had chiseled features, a strong jawline, and piercing honey-colored brown eyes that seemed to see right through her.

Today, he wore a muscle-fit black shirt that accentuated

his broad shoulders and lean physique, along with his typical blue jeans. He looked good in everything.

He wasn't in the office much, usually supervising the larger projects or in the vast greenhouses behind the offices. Whitlock Landscaping supplied its own trees, flowers, and shrubs, so it had to stock a wide variety of plants.

He didn't like being shackled to a desk.

He usually had a weekly one-on-one meeting with the small office staff to inquire about their progress for the week. He liked tangible results. As a social media manager, Cayenne usually urged customers to say where they found out about the business. So far, they had gotten major referrals through her efforts, and she figured she was now a valuable team member.

He smiled at her. "Sage, have a seat."

She hurriedly sat. She had to train herself not to swoon when he smiled. One would think that after dating his son for two years and seeing Bruce every week, she could resist that smile, but it still made her weak in the knees. He had no idea how she felt. She would be mortified if he did.

"So, I was commissioned to do a multimillion-dollar project," Bruce said. "It is an all-inclusive golf resort. The property developers want us to design a large golf course and landscape the entire property, including luxury gardens, walking paths, and multiple themed areas. It's a huge opportunity for Whitlock Landscaping, and it's largely because of the exceptional work you've done marketing us. You deserve every dime I pay you and more."

Sage smiled. "I am glad I am making a difference here at Whitlock Landscaping."

"We could do a series on this project for social media," Bruce said. "The villas are not yet done, but that's okay. The client wants us to start working on the gardens of the newly renovated family house on the other side of the resort. It will remain as a private property and will overlook the golf course."

"Oh wow," Sage nodded. "It sounds pretty, and yes, a series would be a great idea. I could record you and edit the videos from the beginning to the final reveal. That's actually an excellent idea."

Bruce nodded. "I am curious to know if you know the property developer. He shares the same last name as you."

"I am not sure," Sage said. "What's his name?"

"Horace Aubry, the house being renovated is Aubry House."

"Er," Sage was stunned. "I don't know Horace, but I have heard of him. He is my father's younger brother. And I didn't know they had a place called Aubry House."

"Oh, your father," Bruce frowned. "I know all about your father. Will this be a problem? Because if it is, we can call this off."

"Oh no," Sage said. "I would never ask you to do that. I don't know Horace, and maybe he doesn't know me. I don't see why this would change anything."

Bruce smiled. "Very well. I'll work on the design for the house grounds. It's three acres on a hill; it should be fun."

Sage chuckled. "I'll need footage of that, your drawings, and the property. I need some good before shots."

Bruce nodded. "Yes. We start the process on Monday. I hope you don't mind staying over at my farm in St. Ann, at least on weekdays. It would be easier for the men and me not to drive to and from Kingston daily. The men will bunk in the cabins on the farm. You will stay with me at my house."

Sage swallowed. Staying with him? Why did that sound so intimate, and why was she so excited about the prospect?

"Well, er, I have no problem at all," Sage said.

Bruce's eyes twinkled with amusement. "Good to know," he said, leaning back in his chair. "I promise you'll have all the amenities you need there."

Sage nodded, trying to suppress the butterflies in her stomach. "Sounds great."

Bruce's phone buzzed on the table as they settled the final details. He glanced at the screen and frowned slightly. "Excuse me for a moment," he said, standing up and stepping away to take the call.

Sage took a deep breath, allowing herself a moment to absorb everything. Working with Bruce on such a personal project was thrilling, not just because of the professional opportunity but also because of the undeniable chemistry she felt between them. She pushed the thought aside. Focus on the job, she reminded herself.

When Bruce returned, his expression had softened. "Everything's all set then. I'll see you on Monday, Sage."

"Looking forward to it," she replied, shaking his hand. His grip was firm, and for a moment, he held her gaze, making her heart race and her skin tingle where he touched her.

The bridal magazine chose that moment to drop from her nerveless fingers.

He glanced at it and then at her. "I didn't know you and Brian were that serious."

"We aren't," Sage cleared her throat. "Well, I am not serious. What I mean to say is... it's for my sister's wedding."

Bruce raised an eyebrow, a flicker of amusement dancing in his eyes. "Your sister's wedding, huh? Well, that makes more sense."

Sage could feel the heat rising to her cheeks. "Yes, she's getting married in a few months. I'm just helping her out with some ideas."

Bruce nodded, a playful smile curling at the corners of his mouth. "Got it. If you need any tips on venues or anything, let me know. I might know a thing or two about making places look beautiful."

Sage laughed, the tension easing. "We might just take you up on that."

"Great," Bruce said, his tone light but his gaze steady. "So, Monday it is. We'll meet with Horace at Aubry House and see where the week takes us."

"Monday," Sage echoed.

She couldn't wait for Monday. Why wasn't it Monday yet? Anticipation sliced through her as she walked out of his office. What would it be like working so closely with Bruce? Would she reveal her feelings for him? And could she keep her composure?

Chapter Two

Bruce tapped his fingers in the middle of his diary when Sage left his office. His social life would be busy this weekend, which was a welcome change. These days, he was so busy with back-to-back jobs that his social interactions had taken a back seat to work.

Tonight, he had to attend a garden party that Ian Greaves, his buddy from college, was throwing to show off his newly completed home in the hills. Bruce had designed the landscape, and he was quite proud of his work with Ian's terraced gardens.

He would suffer through the small talk and pleasantries tonight just to hear the compliments about the finished work and pick up another job or two while he was at it. This event he would attend alone.

And then, on Saturday evening, he had a date. His first date in months, four months to be exact. He had quite inexplicably lost his appetite for female companionship. His long-standing relationship with Melissa had ended when she migrated a few months ago, and he had not replaced her.

His date with Lacy Logan was supposed to end his self-inflicted aloneness and take his mind off Sage Aubry. In fact, he had accepted Lacy's casual invite to watch a movie or something this weekend because she had more than a passing resemblance to Sage.

Since he met Sage last year, she had started to pop up in his head at the most inconvenient times.

He had to get her out of his head. It was becoming ridiculous. He would never in a million years have thought that he would be one of those men who would be attracted to his son's girlfriend. These days, whenever he saw Sage, his eyes lingered, his heart quickened, and his pulse leaped. His whole body reacted to her.

What was going on? From the first moment he had met her, he had been like this. He had just been successful at hiding it.

He had expected this reaction to pass. He had been waiting for it to subside. Sage was not a potential partner. She was his son's girlfriend, and Brian seemed to love her very much.

Bruce's feelings were way out of line, but only he knew about them, and he would keep it that way. Neither Sage nor Brian would ever know.

He got up and stretched. He needed to go to his house, which was nearby, and get ready for the party. He glanced at the clock; it was nearly four o'clock. If he left the office in the next few minutes, traffic would not be so bad.

He grabbed his keys and picked up his knapsack. The admin offices were at the back of the building; they had a kitchen/dining room, a boardroom, and the offices. His office manager, Jackie Landry, was on the phone when he walked by her office.

He stopped. "Everything set for Monday?" he asked at her office door.

"Yes," Jackie covered the phone, "everything is set for you. Our other project managers, however, are scrambling to cover the other jobs you are leaving for the Aubry one."

"I know," Bruce nodded. "It will work itself out. A couple of jobs are finishing up this month, so my input is not needed as much. See you next Friday when I get back."

"Actually, I will see you before that," Jackie covered the phone. "Carl and I were also invited to the party this evening. He is on the phone now; he doesn't know what to wear to a garden party. What are you wearing?"

"I planned to wear a black polo shirt and jeans." Bruce shrugged. "Did he hear something different?"

"Nope," Jackie said. "I think the word 'garden' before the party confuses him. He was thinking of a floral shirt."

"That could work, too," Bruce chuckled. "See you later."

Jackie nodded and went back to the conversation with her husband.

Carl was the reason he had hired Jackie. Twelve years ago, when his business had taken off like it had wings, he had needed someone to organize his operation. Carl, his lawyer and close family friend, had suggested that he hire his wife.

Jackie had quit her corporate job as a human resource manager to be a stay-at-home mom. Carl had called him and begged him to hire her.

"Now that the girls are at school, she has nothing to do with her time, and she wanders around the house aimlessly. She sometimes comes to the office and is driving my current office manager crazy. Hire Jackie; you won't regret it."

And he hadn't, not even once. Bruce smiled to himself.

Jackie had other links to his family, too. Apart from being Carl's wife, she was the aunt to Natalia Henderson, Brian's childhood friend and high school sweetheart. They had all thought that Brian and Natalia would have stayed together; they were so close.

But that relationship had fizzled out when they went to different universities. And when Brian met Sage.

He still remembered when Brian had called him, almost beside himself with joy. "Dad, the prettiest girl at school, sat beside me in class today. I asked her out, and she said yes."

Bruce remembered chuckling, "Good for you, Brian."

"No, she is not the prettiest girl at school," Brian said. "She is the prettiest girl in the world. Natalia is going to weep when she sees her."

"You are not dating this girl to make Natalia jealous, are you?" Bruce had asked.

"Of course I am, that's a part of it," Brian had said, "but I really can't believe that she is going out with me. When you see her, you'll know what I mean."

****

"**O**h, Bruce," Sage said behind him breathlessly as if she were running.

Bruce spun around and stopped just before reaching his car. Yes, he had found out exactly what Brian had meant. Sage was indeed pretty and completely nonchalant about it.

He remembered complimenting her the first time they had met, and she had blushed like crazy and responded quite self-deprecatingly.

"In my family, I am the ugly duckling in a house of swans. Even my name is the least exciting of the spices. My grandmother is Rosemary, my mother is Anise, my sisters are Cinnamon and Cayenne, and I am good old-fashioned Sage, the herb they wheel out when they want to clean a room."

He had laughed heartily; she had a quirky sense of humor.

"That's not exactly true," he corrected her. "As a landscaper, I find sage to be a terrific herb and so versatile. It adds a wonderful texture and aroma to any garden, and I use it in so many dishes. I did a garden the other day for a client, and she requested a sage border. She said she drank sage tea every day because her dentist recommended it. Apparently, it's one of the popular herbs in dentistry, as it targets pain, inflammation, and bad breath, and also exerts antibacterial and wound-healing properties."

"What?" Sage looked at him, clearly surprised.

"I could go on and on about how incredible sage is," Bruce said. "If you don't mind me asking, what's your middle name?"

"Amethyst," Sage said.

"Now that's a thoughtful pairing of names," Bruce said. "Amethyst, the purple quartz, usually symbolizes deep love, happiness, humility, sincerity, and wealth."

Sage giggled, the sound light and melodic, making Bruce's heart swell. "Well, I never thought of it that way. Maybe I'm not so boring after all."

Bruce smiled warmly. "You're definitely not boring, Sage. At least Brian doesn't seem to think so. Whose idea was it to pair a spice and a stone name? It's brilliant."

"It's a family tradition," Sage said. "My sisters' names are Cinnamon Jade and Cayenne Onyx."

Now, standing by his car, waiting for her to catch up, Bruce replayed that conversation in his mind.

"You walk so fast," Sage said, meeting up with him and panting a little. "One minute you were at Jackie's office, and the next you are here."

"What's wrong?" he asked.

"Nothing is wrong," Sage said. "I just remembered I'll have to ask you for a lift on Monday. I am between cars at the moment. According to the dealer, my new car will not be here for at least two months, and I can't take my sister's car out of town for a whole week."

"What happened to your old car?" Bruce raised an eyebrow. He wasn't sure he liked the idea of them having long, uninterrupted times together with nothing to do but talk. It wouldn't help him with his quest to not get closer.

Sage said, "I sold it to a friend. I thought I could easily replace it, but then I saw that they had an electric version, and I was intrigued. So I ordered one, but it will take a while to arrive. I was quite fine waiting. I only come to the offices once a week when you are here anyway."

Bruce nodded. "Okay, I'll pick you up at the crack of dawn Monday. Send me your address."

Sage nodded. "What time is the crack of dawn?"

Bruce smiled. "Five-thirty."

"Okay. See you Monday."

She turned back and walked towards the office, and Bruce tried not to admire how well-proportioned her body was. She was tall and curvy in all the right places.

You will be going out tomorrow evening with a more age-appropriate version of Sage, his inner voice reminded him. Lacy Lopez could be Sage's close family member. They had the same russet-colored curly hair, light brown eyes, and sun-kissed caramel-smooth skin. They both glowed with an inner radiance that was impossible to ignore.

But Lacy wasn't Sage. And he had niggling doubts that a years-long attraction to his son's girlfriend would disappear overnight with Lacy. But one could hope.

Chapter Three

Sage read Cayenne's directions for the fifth time while slowly crawling through the neighborhood. The address said: 102 Spring Street. Turn left at the guinep tree, then right at the grey stone wall, and follow the path until you see the red mailbox. Sage sighed; the directions seemed straightforward, but every tree and wall looked similar in the fading light of dusk.

She checked to make sure she hadn't missed a turn. The guinep tree had been easy enough to spot, its distinctive fruits dangling like ornaments, but the grey stone wall had been trickier. The custom dress designer apparently operated out of her garage. She had given up trying to read the numbers on the gates; not everybody displayed them prominently, and all the mailboxes were red.

Sage was getting antsy. She didn't want her design to be the last one in the Battle of the Dresses competition.

She finally spotted her grandmother's, Cinnamon's, and

Anise's cars. It was the right place! They were all there and accounted for, probably shoving their dresses ideas down Cayenne's throat.

She pulled over and parked, stepping out into the warm, humid evening air. She could hear the laughter as she walked up the brick path to the garage that was converted into a dressmaker's store. The dressmaker, Jada, was Anise's friend who sewed and designed all her custom clothes. Admittedly, the custom pieces looked indistinguishable from the mass-produced stuff she got from the store. Still, Sage had doubts about how good Jada would be with wedding wear.

She didn't need to be in any doubt, she realized when she stepped into the converted garage. The space was transformed into an elegant boutique, with racks of luxurious fabrics, mannequins draped in half-finished gowns, and a large worktable cluttered with sewing tools and sketches. The soft glow of overhead lights highlighted the meticulous details on the dresses, dispelling any of Sage's previous doubts.

Everybody was gathered around a large idea board. Jada was at the center of it all. She was a tall woman, even taller than Rosemary and Anise, who were at least six feet tall themselves. Her hair was cleanly shaved. She had a nicely shaped head. Sage wondered idly if she would be brave enough to shave off her hair like that. It was a style she had found herself fantasizing about the longer her hair got.

Jada pinned a sketch to the board, and everybody stood back looking at it.

"I am here!" Sage interrupted their contemplation.

"Finally! The last contender has arrived," Jada said, looking around with a playful wink. "Come in, Sage. We've been waiting for you."

"What took you so long?" Cinnamon asked.

"Traffic," Sage said. "And when I got here, I couldn't find the place with the red mailbox. Did you know there are at least five red mailboxes on this side of the road?"

Cayenne chuckled. "They are not deep red like Jada's."

"I was just about to leave without seeing your design," Rosemary said, glancing at her watch. "I am on the way to Ian Greaves' garden party. I am the MC for the evening."

"Oh," Sage said. "I don't want you to be late, Nana. Well, here it is, the design."

Jada took it from her and pinned it on the board.

"The first one is Anise's, the second is Rosemary's, the third is Cinnamon's, and the last is yours, Sage," Jada said. "They are lovely."

They all stood back and looked at the four designs.

"I will go with the popular vote," Cayenne added. "I liked them all when you sent me the ideas. I liked Nana's because of the lace bell sleeves; it's so elegant and classic. I love the boat neck in Mom's design with the geometric patterns and the gold insets in the front."

"It is gorgeous," Sage whistled.

"Thank you," Anise blushed slightly. "I think Cayenne would look good in something contemporary yet sophisticated."

Cayenne nodded. "I love the transparent design on the back of Cinnamon's dress and the shape of Sage's."

"I think that shape would look perfect on you," Sage murmured. "The fishtail look will also suit your location by the beach."

"True," Cayenne nodded.

"Why choose?" Jada suggested. "Why not incorporate elements from all the designs? That way, everyone's vision is part of the final creation. I can do a mash-up of all the designs: lace bell sleeves, boat neck, carrying the lace panel to the back, and making it a fishtail shape.”

There was a moment of silence as the idea sank in. Then, one by one, they all started to nod in agreement.

“That’s a fantastic idea,” Rosemary said, her eyes lighting up. “We can combine the best features of each design.”

“And make something truly special,” Anise added.

“Look what can happen when all the spices work together,” Jada smiled warmly. “Alright then, it's settled. I’ll merge the designs and send it to you for your approval, Cayenne. If you give me the go-ahead, we can meet again to choose materials and that sort of thing.”

“Oh, that’s great,” Cayenne said.

“I have to run,” Rosemary said. “But I am looking forward to seeing the final product.”

“Me too,” Cinnamon grabbed her bag. “I promised Jax I would meet him at the Wilde Building after this. We are having a long weekend together with no children around.”

“VJ is just one little boy!” Anise protested.

“He feels like ten little boys,” Cinnamon chuckled. “And whoever coined the term 'terrible twos' knew about him and was describing him to a T. Where did the cute little baby stage go? My little cutie is a sweet, adorable monster.”

“So, who is staying with him?” Anise asked.

“His other grandmother,” Cinnamon said. “Devina is keeping him for the weekend. She has been begging to have him for an extended time. I bet she won't make that offer again after this weekend.”

“My grandson is no trouble at all,” Anise said. “I could keep him.”

Cinnamon grinned. “Mom, I know you would have him live with you, but you need to give Devina some time with him, too. Bye, guys.” She kissed them and left.

“Well,” Anise huffed, “I could have done some babysitting

this weekend. I have nothing on my calendar. I am coming home with you two. We haven't had a girls' weekend in months!"

Sage chuckled. "It will just be me and you. Cayenne spends most of her time next door; she's all but moved over."

"True," Cayenne nodded. "Lance had a tiring couple of weeks. We were just going to relax this weekend."

"That's not a problem," Anise said. "I haven't had a chance to catch up with my youngest. We'll make it a thing: cook food, go to the spa, catch a movie, and maybe check out the jazz concert Sunday evening at Hope Gardens."

Sage clapped her hands. "Sounds like the weekend is going to be lit."

Chapter Four

It did start out that way. Anise cooked them supper. It was a simple spread: garlic bread, roasted beef, and a fresh garden salad with a light vinaigrette. The aroma of the roasted beef filled the room, mingling with the scent of freshly baked garlic bread. It smelled so good that Lance came over and hung out with them. They watched a movie, and Sage slept in late the next day.

"Rise and shine," Anise knocked on her door. "I didn't want to disturb you, but I booked a spa treatment for us at one o'clock, and then we have to leave for a movie. I have been dying to watch Dawn of Day. It's about an undercover nun."

"It sounds like a rip-off of Sister Act with Whoopi Goldberg," Sage blinked at her mother blearily. "What are you wearing?"

Anise wore a seventies-inspired pink and green dress, platform shoes, and a vibrant pink headband over a shoulder-length wig with barrel curls.

"I am in my seventies era," Anise spun around.

"You look like you could star in Grease," Sage chuckled. "I like the twenty-first-century era, thank you very much. I'll be getting up; a spa treatment sounds amazing. I could use some relaxation before St. Ann next week."

"What's happening in St. Ann?" Anise asked.

"My boss got a contract for a big project. He wants me to document the process and use it as one long infomercial."

"Oh," Anise looked at her, "I feel there is more. You look guilty."

"It's for Aubry House," Sage whispered. "I didn't want to tell you." She pulled the sheet over her head.

"Aubry House?" Anise sat on the bed. "The house of sin, the den of iniquity, the petri dish of scandal and shame. Why on earth would your boss want to do any work there?"

Sage groaned. "Because it is a good business move. Why wouldn't he take it? Why do you call it the den of iniquity?"

Anise shrugged. "Actually, those were your father's words, not mine. He found living there with his parents difficult. He never said why. He left as soon as he could. He said he saw and experienced things there that he couldn't talk about, and if he could say that and was so messed up himself, I assume what happened there was really bad."

Sage removed the sheet from her head. "I wonder what it could be? What do you know about the Aubrys?"

Anise sighed. "I don't know much about them. Paul and I married at a registrar's office; he didn't invite anyone from his family. It was while I was pregnant with Cayenne that I learned he had siblings. I met Donna, his older sister, and his younger brother, Horace. They came to discuss a family matter. After they left, Paul said it was about Aubry House—the family house that his mother had lived in until her death. It was left to the three of them equally in her will when she died."

"She's dead?" Sage asked.

"Yes, your grandparents are gone to the great beyond," Anise nodded solemnly. "I never met any of them, though. Paul didn't talk about his family much."

"Tell me about Paul," Sage said eagerly.

Anise sighed. "And here I was having a good day."

"I don't know anything about my father or his family," Sage said. "It has always fascinated me. I once tried doing a search on the internet, but I came up with nothing."

Anise sighed again. "I guess it is only fair that you know some things. People are generally curious about their family. I was curious about the Greystones when I discovered Richard Greystone was my father."

"So, how did you two meet?" Sage jumped up out of bed. Anise got up and watched her as she spread out her things.

"Sculpting class at the community college," Anise said. "I saw the advertisement on the school noticeboard. I was doing my associate's degree in criminal justice then but wanted to do something creative as well."

"I didn't know you did criminal justice," Sage frowned.

"I wanted to be a policewoman or something in social work," Anise said. "I always had fantasies of taking down the bad guys, especially the child abusers."

"With your history, that's understandable," Sage said.

"Yes," Anise nodded. "And it was my history that, funnily enough, attracted Paul to me. I was a child abuse victim, and he was an abuser. Paul used to ask me to tell him my abuse story in detail. At first I thought it was sweet—finally, I had someone I could talk to who wasn't repulsed by hearing my side of the story and was never tired of me going on and on about it."

"But looking back," she continued, "he wasn't interested in my story because he cared. It aroused him. My childhood trauma was a turn-on for him. He loved hearing my story and urged me to describe all the gory parts."

"Can we rewind a bit?" Sage said. "How did you meet? What did he say to you?"

"We met in his class," Anise began. "The teacher who got him to guest lecture introduced him as Paul Aubry, one of the greatest sculptors of our generation. Apparently, we were lucky to be breathing the same air as him." Anise chuckled. "I thought he was cute. He was tall—a requirement you know I have because I am six feet tall."

Sage nodded.

"He had brown curly hair, green eyes, and smooth caramel skin. There were no wrinkles in sight. I thought he was much younger. Anyway, I enjoyed his class. And even though he turned out to be an evil son of the devil, he was a good teacher, and he was good-looking."

Sage chuckled. "Son of the devil?"

"I am trying not to swear," Anise shrugged. "I want to call him names so badly, but I am keeping it cute. My therapist said I should use non-abrasive words while telling my story. It will keep me from going into negative territory."

"Fair enough," Sage nodded.

"So anyway," Anise continued, "I was in the middle of class when Grandma Saidie called. Cinnamon had an accident at the daycare. I jumped up, almost knocking over my mold. I hurriedly told Paul that my daughter had an accident at the playground.

"He looked at me fascinated and asked, 'How old are you?'

"Seventeen, I said defiantly. People usually get judgmental when you're a young mother. He didn't seem judgmental, though. He was fascinated."

"'And how old is she? Your daughter?' he asked.

"Four, I said. His eyes took on a dreamy quality."

'You had her at thirteen?'

"I nodded impatiently. He smiled. The man actually smiled and said, 'Call me and let me know how she is doing.'

"He took my number, and I took his and we started corresponding. Of course, he wanted to know why I was such a young mother. I told him I was molested by my father. I ran away, became a prostitute for a couple of months, was rescued by my mother's friend, and went on and on.

"He had found his soul mate. My story was just enough red meat to stoke his attraction. I wasn't as young as he liked, but my past was something he was drawn to.

"He said he wanted to sculpt me. I agreed; we had been talking a lot by then, and I thought I knew him. I started staying with him on the weekends. Grandma Saidie disapproved, but I thought I was in love and didn't care what she said.

"Paul was perfect. He love-bombed me and treated me like a princess; I wanted for nothing, emotionally, sexually, or physically. He suggested that I bring Cinnamon to live with us."

"Thank God you didn't," Sage whispered, horrified.

"If God is Grandma Saidie," Anise said wistfully. "When I suggested it, Grandma Saidie said, 'Not over my dead body. I will not let my great-grand even visit you while you shack up with that man.'

"And so, after that pronouncement—which I duly reported to Paul—he offered to marry me. He said he didn't want to shack up anymore." Anise laughed dryly. "What he meant was that he was desperate for my five-year-old to live with us so that he could give her the Paul Aubry treatment. And marriage was the answer. I was so stupid and naïve that I said yes. I was just happy I was getting married.

"But even after marriage, my grandmother said no. I'm sorry, Anise. I am not giving Cinnamon to you."

Anise sighed, "She said to me one day, Anise, listen, there is something about Paul I can't put into words, but it makes me afraid for you. I felt the same way about your mother's husband. They have the same aura. If you want to ignore me like your mother did, go ahead, but you see what her ignorance did to you. Do you want that for Cinnamon?"

"I thought she was being overly cautious about Paul for nothing. He was the best, and in my young, naïve opinion, she didn't know what she was talking about."

Anise sat down on the bed and looked across at Sage. "But I trusted her; she was there for me even when my own mother was not. She didn't need to be told twice that I was molested. I had run to her to escape them, and she protected me like a fierce bulldog.

"If you are serious about any man, take him to Grandma Saidie to vet. She has a sixth sense about people."

Sage nodded.

"Are you going to bathe?" Anise asked. "We have a spa appointment."

"I wanted to hear more," Sage said. "You never talk about this stuff, and it's intriguing. I feel as if I know you better."

"I know," Anise said. "People would rather talk about their triumphs than their failures."

"You weren't a failure," Sage said. "You were a victim."

"Maybe not a failure, but I did let myself down. I should have seen Paul a mile away," Anise said. "But I was so young, naïve, and desperate for what I thought was love. Any man who keeps you away from his family rushes the relationship, pushes for intimacy too quickly, monitors your activities like he's some sort of drill sergeant, refuses to respect your boundaries, acts like you asked him if he committed murder just because you ask about his past relationships, and makes you feel like you're always walking on eggshells—those are all huge red flags. But back then, I ignored them. I wanted to believe in the fairytale, not the reality.

"I am so happy you will never have to deal with that; you and Brian make such a cute couple."

Sage cleared her throat. "About that…"

"You broke up?" Anise widened her eyes. "When?"

"We aren't officially broken up," Sage sighed. "I want to, but he doesn't."

"I see," Anise nodded.

"I like his father," Sage said. "I mean, I really, really, really like him."

Anise chuckled. "I can see the appeal. Bruce Whitlock is fine."

"You know Brian's father?" Sage narrowed her eyes. "You didn't date him, did you?"

"No, I didn't date him," Anise raised an eyebrow. "Do you think I date everybody in this town? And for your information, I saw Bruce when he was working on a golf course for a friend of mine."

"Oh," Sage grimaced. "It seems like you date everybody in town."

"Well, I don't," Anise said. "Besides, the papers exaggerate things. If I take a smiling picture with a guy, he's my latest victim. The truth is sometimes quite far from the reports. I can still count on my fingers and toes the number of relationships I've had over the years. It's not that much."

"Good for you," Sage said. "You never let us meet them. I'll take your word for it."

"And I never will," Anise snorted. "I was not going to

bring any man around my girls. Even though you're all adults, I still won't do it. If I ever introduce you to someone, it's because I am super sure he will be permanent in my life. Otherwise, nope, not happening."

Sage grinned. "Okay."

"I've had too many unsuccessful relationships," Anise sighed. "I should write a book—a cautionary tale to young women trying to find love in this era."

"You should do it," Sage said. "I'd read it."

"Hmmm," Anise mused, "maybe I should make it fictional and do a series. And change names so that no one knows who I am talking about. The main protagonist would have a spice first name and maybe a stone last name. I would lay it all out. I would shroud some relationships in secrecy like the one I had with a particular international musician."

Sage giggled. "Luke Mallory, who looks like Santa Claus."

"He popped Viagra like it was going out of style, and it still didn't help," Anise said sadly. "It made him very self-conscious about his... situation."

Sage laughed. "Oh, Ma, tell me more."

"No," Anise said, "I have tattled enough."

"You've been in several age-gap relationships, both ways. I know about you and Luke Mallory and that old banker guy. Then there was the basketball player," Sage said interestedly. "What do you think about the chance of success for those relationships?"

"Well," Anise mused, "when I'm older in the relationship, I tend to be more nurturing. I find myself guiding and supporting my partner more, which can be exhausting. I always tell myself I don't want to be any man's mother. I usually give the speech, 'I am a girlfriend, not your mother. I have a daughter your age, and she is more mature than this.'"

Sage chuckled. "And what about when you're the younger one?"

Anise grinned. "When I'm the younger one, it's a different dynamic. There's a risk of feeling overshadowed or not taken seriously. It's easy to fall into a pattern where the older guy takes charge and starts treating me like a child or slightly less than."

"I usually end up giving the speech," Anise continued. "'Listen, hello, I am an independent woman. I make my own money, I own my house, I despise my father, and I don't want another.' The ones who can't take the fathering attitude out of their system can get really stifling after a while."

Sage leaned on the wall. "What do you think makes these relationships work or fail?"

Anise took a deep breath. "Mutual respect. Communication. Both partners need to feel valued and heard. It's also important to have shared goals and interests so the age difference doesn't become a source of constant tension. And, honestly, you both need to be prepared for the challenges that come with being at different life stages."

"Bruce is how much older?" Anise asked.

"Eighteen years," Sage said.

Anise nodded. "That's not that bad, in my opinion. But what do I know? I dated a guy thirty years older."

"Thirty?" Sage widened her eyes. "that's grandfather territory."

Anise laughed. "I tend to gravitate toward older men. My therapist says I have daddy issues."

Sage raised an eyebrow. "Daddy issues. I can see that being a problem for you, but not for me. I never had a daddy to have issues about."

"True," Anise nodded. "Hence the reason why I never

brought any men around. When there's no daddy, there ain't no issues."

Sage chuckled.

"For me personally, daddy issues aside," Anise said, "I do like the stability and maturity that older men bring to a relationship. It's not always about some deep-seated psychological need. Sometimes, it's just about finding someone who complements you in the right ways."

Sage nodded slowly. "I get that. But what about the judgment from others? Doesn't it get tiring?"

"I never let people's opinions affect anything I do," Anise shrugged. "People will always have something to say, don't they? But at the end of the day, it's about what makes you happy. If an older guy treats you well and you feel good about the relationship, then that's what matters."

Sage smiled. "You're right. You know, Mom, sometimes you can be so wise. I actually like you as a person."

Anise grinned. "Why, thank you. That means a lot."

"So, tell me about your much older man friend—the one who could be your grandfather."

"I was in my late twenties," Anise said. "He wasn't bad—better than the men in my age group I've dated before and since. We broke up because he wanted someone more flexible with their time and available whenever he crooked his fingers. And I had my own things going on. He wasn't used to my type of woman. After several arguments about my inflexibility, I realized that I just didn't want to be flexible for him."

"Tell me more about the banker guy?" Sage mused. "What's his name again? Escovito? His family actually owns the bank."

"I don't kiss and tell," Anise said. "Will you go and get ready?"

"So, what about your latest relationship?" Sage asked. "The guy you told Cayenne about."

"I mentioned to your sister that I was happy and in a good place with a man I could see myself with for the foreseeable future. Unfortunately, it didn't work out." Anise shrugged. "I'm not mad about it. The hunt continues for Mr. Right. I may never find him, and you know what? I feel I'm okay with that at this stage in my life. Maybe it's time to give singleness a try. It's not that bad. I can focus on my own passions, travel, and spend time with the people who matter most to me. Sometimes, being single offers a kind of freedom and clarity that relationships don't."

Sage nodded thoughtfully. "I get that. It's about finding happiness in your own company, right?"

"Exactly," Anise said. "And if the right person comes along, great. If not, I still have a fulfilling life. It's a win-win situation."

Sage smiled warmly at her mother. "I'm glad you're in a good place, Mom. You deserve it."

Anise returned the smile, her eyes twinkling with affection. "Thanks, sweetheart. Now, let's get moving. We've got a lot to do today."

Chapter Five

Bruce was sitting in the back of the movie theater with Lacy when he saw Sage walk in with another woman, whom he assumed was one of her sisters. They sat three rows ahead of him. She looked gorgeous and glowing in shorts and a tube top. Her hair was out, cascading over her shoulders and covering her top.

Bruce couldn't take his eyes off her. It was the first time he had seen her dressed so casually and with her hair out.

Lacy leaned over to him and whispered, "That's Anise Cooper and her daughter. I don't know which one."

"Sage," Bruce replied. "Her name is Sage. She works with me. I thought her mother was her sister or something."

"Anise had them when she was young," Lacy said. "And she takes care of herself. I've been waiting for years for her to show some aging and sagging or gain some weight and look like a barrel."

Bruce chuckled. "Women who look like Anise don't

decline; they get more graceful with age."

"More's the pity," Lacy snorted.

"What's the story with you and Anise?" Bruce asked.

"It's a long one and not interesting," Lacy shrugged. "Needless to say, she won, and I have resented her ever since. Though the prize is with neither of us at the moment, so the war did not really matter."

Bruce chuckled.

Sage and Anise were laughing at something, their heads close together. They were completely absorbed in their own world and oblivious to being gossiped about.

Lacy nudged him gently. "People say I resemble Sage, and the other one—I think her name is Pepper. What do you think?"

Bruce forced a smile. "Well, yes… a little bit, I guess."

Lacy chuckled. "I wouldn't mind if I discover that I'm a long-lost sister. Despite his stint in jail, I hear that Paul Aubry is still as rich as ever, even more so since then."

Bruce cleared his throat. Lacy was beginning to annoy him. She mostly talked about money, looks, and the number of high-profile men she had dated. After nearly thirty minutes in her presence, he decided to drop her home after the movie and lose her number.

She may resemble Sage, but he wasn't attracted to her— not even a teensy bit. He would snooze through the movie; he would have preferred to watch something other than Dawn of Day. But Lacy was excited to see it.

He wondered if Sage liked it.

The movie started, but Bruce found it hard to focus. His mind drifted to Sage; he stared at the back of her head more than he did on the movie screen.

He had to get himself under control. They would be working together for the next couple of weeks, closer than they had ever worked before.

Sage was dating his son. He couldn't forget that.

His mind wandered to his conversation with Brian just a year ago after his last exam.

"So, what's next?" Bruce had asked while getting ready for work. Brian had come up to the main house and was rifling through his fridge.

Brian lived downstairs on the first floor of the Kingston house. He had his own apartment and could come and go as he pleased, and they needn't be in each other's space.

When Bruce bought the place, the previous owners had used the downstairs as a rental. He wrestled with the idea of living with tenants and eventually settled on keeping the space for visiting family and friends. Brian commandeered it as his own when he moved to Kingston to live with him after high school.

"I have a summer job," Brian said, taking out his leftover dinner from the night before. "What's this?"

"Curried goat and fried chicken," Bruce said. "I ate out last night."

"Mmm," Brian said, putting the plate into the microwave. "It smells yum."

Bruce smiled. "So you haven't done groceries yet?"

"No," Brian shrugged, "but your pantry is well-stocked. I think I'm going to get a few items."

"Do your own shopping," Bruce said.

"But you have groceries enough for a dozen people," Brian protested. "Why can't I share with you?"

"Because you need to be responsible. Shopping in my pantry is a budget shortcut I won't encourage. I work quite hard to prevent you from being a spoiled brat."

Brian rolled his eyes. "So now am I going to hear stories about how when you were my age, you had already started a business, lived alone, and had a three-year-old son to look after? And that you weren't getting handouts from your parents?"

Bruce laughed. "Actually, I was going to ask you when did you pick up a summer job and congratulate you for taking the initiative to find one in the first place."

"Yes, I got a summer job with Uncle Garrick. Natalia will be working there for the summer, too."

"Your obsession with her will never end," Bruce said. I thought you would have moved on after your so-called breakup."

"My obsession with her has ended," Brian protested.

"You two still talking?" Bruce asked skeptically.

"Yes," Brian nodded. "She is still my friend. That will never change."

"Okay, fair enough," Bruce said. "What about your girlfriend, Sage?"

"Sage is great. That's the beauty of this," Brian grinned. "Natalia is extremely jealous of Sage. It's a sight to see. She growls when I say her name. I have this picture of Sage in my wallet; she found it and ripped it up."

"So you plan to flaunt your relationship with Sage to make Natalia seethe?"

"That's right," Brian nodded.

"That's quite immature," Bruce said. "You know what I think?"

"What?" Brian frowned.

"You still have feelings for Natalia, and she still has feelings for you," Bruce said. "You are using Sage to make her jealous. This won't end well for one of you in this love triangle. And I'm betting it's not going to be Sage."

"I love Sage!" Brian said. "I really do! And I swear I'm not using her to make Natalia jealous. It may have started out that way when Natalia started seeing Shane Magnus. I really, really dislike that guy."

"But Sage is so sweet, down-to-earth, and grounded. She acts far older than me sometimes, and I must admit that irks me a bit. And sometimes, I wish we had more chemistry. I wish she felt passionate about me, you know what I mean?"

Bruce nodded. "I think I do."

"No," Brian said, "you don't understand. Women are always tripping over you and making fools of themselves. I wish Sage would act like that over me. I want her to be unable to help herself around me. I want her to lose control."

Bruce frowned. "Why?"

Brian sighed and ran a hand through his hair. "Because it makes me feel wanted. It makes me feel... alive. I feel a rush when Natalia gets jealous. For me it's confirmation that she still cares, and that I matter."

Bruce shook his head slowly. "That's not love, Brian. That's just ego. Love isn't about someone losing control over you. It's about mutual respect, understanding, and a deep connection. Do you have that with Sage?"

Brian hesitated. "I think so. I mean, she's always there for me, listens, and is supportive."

"But do you feel connected to her on a deeper level? Beyond just wanting her to be jealous or passionate?"

Brian looked away, his face conflicted. "I don't know. Maybe I don't."

Bruce leaned forward. "If you don't figure this out, you'll hurt Sage. And probably yourself, too. You need to be honest with her and yourself about what you want."

Brian nodded slowly. "I guess you're right. I just... I just want to feel something real, you know?"

"Then start by being real," Bruce said. "With Sage, with Natalia, and most importantly, with yourself. It's the only way any of this will end well."

He must have dozed off during the movie. Lacy poked him in his side. "It's over."

Bruce blinked rapidly. "Oh, it is. How was it?"

Lacy gave him a sour look. "It was great!"

"Sorry," Bruce said wryly.

"Apology accepted." Lacy tucked her hand into his as they walked out of the theater. "You know what I'm in the mood for?"

"What?" Bruce asked lazily.

"An ice cream sundae," Lacy said with a sly smile. "You can lick it all off my belly. We can get it to go and then head to your place."

"My place?" Bruce said, trying to extricate himself from Lacy. "I don't lick anything off anyone on the first date, second or the third. I like to get to know a woman first."

"Wise words," Anise Cooper said from behind them. "Hello, Bruce. I dragged my daughter over here to introduce us."

Bruce managed to pull away from Lacy. "Oh, hello."

Anise held out her hand to shake his. "I am Anise Cooper, Sage's mother."

Sage waved to him. "Hi, Bruce."

"Hi, Sage," he smiled. "Nice to meet you, Anise."

Lacy looked annoyed. "Anise."

"Lacy," Anise chuckled.

"How do you know each other?" Sage asked curiously.

"We were both dating the same guy at one point," Anise said. "And I told him to choose me or her. He chose me. But unfortunately, he couldn't be faithful to save his life, so I dumped him."

"Bruce is not interested in your story," Lacy said hurriedly. "Let's go, Bruce."

Bruce glanced at Sage. "See you tomorrow at the crack of dawn."

Sage nodded, looking like she was holding back a laugh.

Chapter Six

When Bruce came to pick her up at five, it was drizzling. The streetlights were still on, and the townhouse complex was quiet. It felt like the whole of Kingston was still.

"So this is the time," she whispered as Bruce helped her with her bag, "when the city actually sleeps."

Bruce chuckled quietly. "This city never sleeps. I passed newspaper vendors at the stoplights, people cleaning the roads, and a few scantily dressed ladies hanging around the corners of certain buildings."

She smiled faintly. "I guess I never noticed. I am never awake at this hour."

Bruce nodded as he closed the trunk. "You'll get used to it in the coming months. This is when we'll get started, just before daybreak and before the heat of the day kicks in. If you really want to get authentic footage."

"I do want to get authentic footage," Sage said eagerly. "I cannot wait to get started."

They got into the car, the sound of rain pattering softly on the roof. She glanced out the window, watching the faint glow of the streetlights blur through the drizzle. She hadn't fully woken up yet. She had been thinking about Bruce all night, tossing and turning, feeling jealous about him and Lacy Lopez.

Her mother sniffed at her before she left last night. "They aren't serious. Didn't you hear what he said to Lacy? That man is a keeper. He is a relationship kind of guy—the kind who takes his time getting to know a woman who is interested in long-term—the marrying kind. If he is in love, he will propose in a heartbeat. He is not one to waste time."

"So, how was your weekend?" Bruce asked as he started the car and pulled out onto the wet streets.

Sage snapped back to the present. "Good. Great, actually. It's always nice to hang out with my mom. We don't do much of that lately; she is so taken up with her grandson. But this weekend, she told me things about herself I have never heard. I appreciate that."

Bruce smiled. "That's great."

"How was your weekend?" Sage asked.

"It was filled with social engagements. It was a nice change of pace," Bruce replied. He slowed down at the stoplight and looked at her. "Did you like the movie yesterday?"

"It was okay," Sage shrugged. "My mom wanted to watch it, and I just tagged along."

"It was the same for me," Bruce nodded. "Lacy wanted to watch it. I think I slept through half of it."

"Lacy Lopez," Sage said. "My mother said she is a pain in the rear end and that I should tell you to run away and never look back."

Bruce laughed. "I kind of figured that out on my own. We met completely by chance. I went to an event; she was the coordinator. She was quite chirpy and outgoing, and I liked her then. When she asked me on a date, I thought she looked harmless enough, so I said yes. I saw you trying not to laugh at me yesterday."

Sage grinned. "You looked like you were trapped."

"She came on too strong," Bruce grimaced. "I thought men were the only ones who moved at hyper speed, oversexualized everything, and acted thirsty. I know women can be like that, but I had never met one."

"There are exceptions to every rule," Sage said. "Lacy is an outlier."

Bruce laughed. "And not to my taste. I won't be seeing her again."

Sage wanted to ask him about his taste in women, what kind of movies he liked, what books and music he enjoyed, and his interests in general. But she feared that he might think she was too inquisitive. Another thing she was super curious about was his current relationship with Brian's mother.

Brian had said his mother was not in the picture; he barely knew her. In fact, he had only met her once. She currently lived in the UK and didn't have a motherly bone in her body.

What had attracted Bruce to her in the first place? Sage wondered.

She was curious about Bruce and all his relationships; it was all swirling around in her head.

"What are you thinking?" he asked after nearly ten minutes of silence.

"You don't want to know; you'll think I am nosy," Sage responded.

"I probably won't think that," Bruce said. "Give it a shot; ask me anything."

"I was thinking about Brian's mother," Sage murmured.

"Ansara Miraj," Bruce looked across at Sage. "What about her?"

"I like her name," Sage said. "What attracted you to her? How did it feel becoming a parent at eighteen?"

"Ansara and I weren't a romance story; we weren't teenage sweethearts who held hands and kissed in the dark and made impossible promises to each other. I was a horny teenager. I wanted to lose my virginity before I turned eighteen," Bruce said bluntly. "Ansara was a girl who would be up for anything. All the boys talked about her and her willingness to make their dreams come true.

"She was pretty and available and was up for anything, and she was sending hints that she liked me. So one day, we had sex at the back of the school while a concert was going on. It lasted about seven minutes."

Sage gasped. "That's specific."

Bruce grinned. "There was a live band; the singer was doing a gospel medley, and he performed three songs back-to-back. The condom broke. I wasn't really worried; Ansara said she was on the pill."

"And then when she became pregnant," Bruce continued, "I was almost sure the child would not be mine. I wasn't fretting like several of the other boys. I used a condom; granted, it had failed, but I still thought I was safe."

"We graduated high school, and I moved on to college. I was in the first year of my civil engineering degree when my parents called me and told me I needed to take a paternity test."

"Why?" Sage asked.

"Up to that point, I had only had one seven-minute encounter with the girl everyone had sex with at school. But they said Ansara had left her newborn baby at their doorstep, and they needed to know if the baby was mine."

Sage gasped. "Wow. She didn't tell you she was going to do that?"

"No," Bruce said. "She didn't have my number but knew where my parents lived. It was hard to miss; they owned one of the largest farms in our community."

"I went home for mid-term holidays and took the test. The baby was mine. I cried so hard. I was inconsolable. My father told me to man up. 'That's what you get for not listening to my advice.' I can still hear him in my head now:

'Bruce, I keep telling you that having sex too early can lead to serious consequences. It's not just about the physical act; it's about responsibility and the readiness to deal with what comes afterward. You need to understand that sex can have emotional and life-changing repercussions.

'If you're not prepared to handle potential outcomes like pregnancy or the responsibilities that come with it, it's better to wait until you are. Didn't I tell you to ensure you're in a stable relationship where you can communicate openly and support each other?

'Didn't I tell you to always practice safe sex and think about the long-term impact your decisions might have? Do you see how you messed up your future and well-being with one impulsive decision that only lasted seven minutes!'"

"You told him about the seven minutes?" Sage chuckled.

"I was so distraught I told them everything," Bruce said. "Then I went to Ansara's house. By then, she was living with an aunt; her parents had kicked her out."

"Ansara was not pleased with the whole situation either. She had been in denial about the pregnancy and had found out too late for a termination. She said if I didn't want the child, she would give it up for adoption."

"I was seriously tempted to say yes, give him up, but my parents said no; they would take care of him. My mother loves babies and doesn't care what circumstances they arrive under. She would have had a dozen children if she could, but she stopped at three because of health complications. I almost killed her when she was pregnant with me, so that's why I am the last of three."

Sage chuckled. "Good for you that your parents were so tolerant. They could have been like Ansara's parents and kicked you out."

"That would never happen," Bruce said. "My parents are good Christian people. And when I say good Christian people, they don't just talk the talk; they walk the walk. They are not judgmental or intolerant in any way; they always lead with love. And that, above all, was a good example for me, my brothers, and Brian."

"So what did you do after discovering he was yours?" Sage asked.

"I went back to college and graduated. My parents did the bulk of the daily parenting. I spent most of Brian's childhood starting the landscape business and trying to establish myself. I took him with me every summer, wherever I was. My son and I have been on some interesting adventures together. The circumstances were not ideal, but I am happy he is here. I love him and would do anything for him within reason."

"Brian said his mother is not interested in being a mother," Sage said.

"She isn't," Bruce said. "She had her own issues growing up. I never knew about them because I didn't know her really; she was just the pretty girl up for anything. I never stopped to think about her as a person. I never really assessed why she would be so hypersexual at her age. That incident with Ansara scared me into being more fastidious with protection and more stringent when choosing my partners. I drum that message into Brian every chance I get.”

“Oh,” Sage murmured. “I think he got it. Unlike the other guys at the university, there was no pressure to have sex with him. We talked a lot. He was easy to be around. I think that's why we were together for so long. I was comfortable with him.”

“For a relationship to work, there needs to be more than comfort,” Bruce said. “Comfort is a good foundation, but you also need trust, communication, shared values, and passion. It's easy to stay in a comfortable situation, but it takes more to build something lasting and meaningful.”

“I know,” Sage nodded. “And that's why I want to break up with him. I've been trying to do so for six months! But Brian absolutely refuses to let go.”

Bruce frowned. “Oh, really?”

“Maybe I shouldn't be admitting this to you,” Sage sighed, “you are his father.”

“You can tell or ask me anything,” Bruce said, looking at her and holding her gaze. “I promise I'll try to be as open and honest with you as possible.”

Sage looked at him. He was so physically beautiful. It was impossible to look away from his piercing brown eyes. She couldn't tell or ask him anything; that would completely disrupt their working relationship.

Her heart did that little dip it usually did when they were in close proximity. “I er… I think…”

Bruce waited her out while she wet her lips nervously.

“You are never usually so reticent to articulate your thoughts.”

“What were we talking about again?” Sage dragged her gaze away from his.

“You've been trying to break up with Brian.”

“Yes,” Sage nodded. “And it's frustrating. He won't listen.

I'm just going to move on and let him get the message."

"Is there someone else?" Bruce asked, slowing to a crawl.

"I can't tell you," Sage said. "It's a secret. I just want to be free of Brian and move on."

"Oh," Bruce looked at her, then went silent.

"What are you thinking?" Sage asked.

"You don't want to know," Bruce said abruptly.

"I'll make you the same offer," Sage said. "You can ask or tell me anything."

"Not this time," Bruce said roughly.

The sun was peeping over the horizon, casting a warm, golden light over the landscape. The silence between them grew heavy and uncomfortable. Sage watched Bruce's profile, trying to gauge his thoughts, but his expression was unreadable.

"Please," Sage said softly, "tell me what you're thinking."

Bruce exhaled slowly, his grip tightening on the steering wheel. "I truly cannot, Sage. Maybe we should change the conversation."

"Maybe we should," Sage sighed.

Chapter Seven

The question of who she loved was running through his mind, even though they chit-chatted all the way into St. Ann. The highway made the journey easier. They stopped for breakfast at a fast-food restaurant and made their way through the rolling green hills of the countryside.

He tried to push the thought away, focusing instead on the scenery passing by the window. Vibrant hues of summer flowers dotted the landscape, and the occasional farmhouse stood as a testament to the area's rural charm.

In an effort to distract himself from Sage's love life and keep things professional, he asked her about the Aubrys.

"I know next to nothing," Sage said. "To be honest with you, I, too, am curious about them. I know I shouldn't be, but I am curious about my father, too."

"That's natural," Bruce said. "You can't take that longing out of most people, even if the father was the worst of the worst."

"He was," Sage snorted. "So, what do you know about them?"

"I've only met Horace Aubry; this is his project. He is an affable person—jovial and down-to-earth. He'll meet us at the house shortly." Bruce slowed down. "This is the beginning of Aubry land. There's the sign." He pointed to a sign that read, 'Private Property. Trespassers Will Be Prosecuted.'

"Oh wow," Sage whispered, looking at the green landscape and the sea beyond. "This is gorgeous."

"It is," Bruce nodded. "I can't wait to get started. Landscaping this place will be a wonderful challenge."

"Wait a minute," Sage murmured. "I should be recording this, and I need drone shots." She rummaged in her bag and pulled out her equipment.

"There'll be enough time for that," Bruce said. "We have a preliminary meeting with Horace; he'll show us around, and tell us his plans for the place. He said he'd meet me at the house. Then, we'll go exploring on our own. I need to start working on a design today; give him a mock-up of what I'm thinking, and if he approves it, we'll start working next week."

Sage nodded briskly.

They drove through what felt like a forest for several minutes. Bruce spotted several mango varieties in the bushes. He discussed them with her and shared little snippets about growing up on a mango farm with his older brothers, Robert and Garrick.

"Brian always talks about his uncle Garrick, the engineer," Sage said.

"Oh yeah," Bruce nodded. "They are close. My brothers had a hand in his upbringing; Brian used to stay with Garrick at his office after school. Brian fell in love with engineering while hanging out there. Eventually, my brother hired both him and Natalia."

"Ah, the fabulous Natalia," Sage smiled. "Brian talks about her a lot. It was a bit intimidating to hear that they remained best friends after breaking up, but none of that bothers me anymore."

"Because you have someone else in mind?" Bruce asked.

"That's right," Sage said.

Bruce nodded grimly. "All of this is a part of life: people break up, make up, and find someone new. Rinse and repeat."

The dense foliage gave way to a wide clearing as big as a football field. It was covered with small shrubs and weeds. Someone had cut a path through the weeds.

Up the hill, on a wide asphalt driveway that had long given way to several potholes, was an impressive Georgian-style house. From afar, it didn't show any wear and tear, but as they drove closer, the ravages of time were evident on the exterior. Several tarpaulins were set up around the front, indicating an active work site.

And there was quite a bit of debris on what was previously the front lawn.

Despite these signs of neglect, the house retained an air of grandeur and stateliness that spoke of its former glory. Bruce couldn't wait to match the gardens to the house. He planned to design something truly spectacular that would complement the Georgian architecture while bringing the grounds back to life.

He parked the car before a hedge of sorry-looking bougainvillea and looked at Sage.

She was wide-eyed, taking it all in. "This place is incredible," she said, her eyes sweeping across the landscape. "I can't believe I am related to the family who owns it."

Bruce nodded. "This is an opportunity to get to know this side of your family. Well, at least certain parts of it."

"Maybe," Sage said.

"I'm going to need pictures of the house and gardens from the old days," Bruce said. "I can see shadows of a spectacular garden. There's a lot of potential here—the gardens, the driveways, the lawns. I will plant some mature palm trees along the driveway; the place calls for a dramatic entrance."

"That mango tree at the entrance to the driveway was dramatic," Sage laughed.

"And filled with termites," Bruce said. "It will be the first thing that goes. I'll maybe plant a jacaranda there instead, on both sides. It will frame the driveway with vivid dark purple blooms."

"Or a lignum vitae tree," Sage said, "which has the same blue-purple flowers but lasts longer and is picturesque all year round."

Bruce smiled. "You know your plants."

"It's my little obsession, and I research like crazy," Sage grinned. "Fair warning: one day, I may start a landscaping business myself and be your competitor."

"I don't doubt you'll do well at it," Bruce said. "Okay, my future competition, let's go."

The front door opened as they approached the house, and Horace Aubry stepped out. He was tall and big-bodied, with salt-and-pepper brown hair and light brown eyes. He had deep laugh lines around his eyes and a warm, welcoming smile that seemed to put everyone at ease. He extended a hand toward Bruce and Sage.

"Welcome, welcome! Come on in," Horace said, his voice friendly. "I hope the drive wasn't too rough."

"Not at all," Bruce replied, shaking Horace's hand firmly.

"Thank you for having us. This place has so much history; it's quite something."

"Indeed, it does," Horace agreed, his eyes twinkling with nostalgia and pride. "The house has been in our family for generations. There's a lot of history here."

Sage looked around, her eyes taking in the intricate details of the old house. "It's beautiful, Mr. Aubry. The architecture, the woodwork—it's all so well-preserved."

"Thank you, Sage. Please, call me Horace," he responded. "I'm not going to pretend that I'm not your uncle. This is as much your history as mine. Our family is troubled, and it has put a wedge between us, but that does not negate the fact that I know of your existence and that we are kin."

Sage cleared her throat. "I didn't want to bring up the connection."

"It's because of the connection that I went with Whitlock Landscaping," Horace said, looking at Bruce. "Of course, I saw your work, and your rates are competitive, Bruce, but the fact that my niece was working for you gave you an extra edge."

"I knew there was some nepotism at work here," Bruce smiled.

"So my father didn't have anything to do with this?" Sage asked. "I was wondering if he had his hand in this somehow."

"Oh no," Horace shook his head. "Since Paul got out of prison, he has been staying at his Bedford property a few miles from here. If you know what I mean, he is working in his studio, exercising, and keeping himself away from temptation."

Sage nodded. "Well, that's a relief."

"I bought out my siblings' shares of the property years ago after our mother died," Horace said. "They were only too willing to sell it to me. Nobody has happy memories of this place."

They stood in the foyer and looked around. The ceilings were high, a grand staircase in the middle added dramatic flair to the entrance. The air was filled with the faint scent of paint. Inside, the work was obviously finished with fine attention to detail.

"So what are you going to do with it?" Bruce asked.

"I will rent it out as a bed and breakfast," Horace said. "At first, I was going to gut it and divide it into apartments, but I did my research and realized that people are interested in staying in old houses and paying top dollar for it. For those who want the experience, this is here."

"The hotel and golf course I'm building nearby will suffice for people who are more into modern accommodations. But I want to keep this private and secluded. I may host events here as well. There is a vast terrace at the back. I'll show you that soon, but let us retire to the library, where the plans are."

"The library is the first place I refurbished when I started. It has its own suite. Back in the day, my father used to practically live down here. We never knew what he did in here. But while refurbishing the place I found some of his journals that date back to his boyhood. He was probably writing his life story. Maybe the journals will give some answers as to what he was doing down here all by himself."

"What time span is childhood?" Sage asked.

"Late 1930s," Horace shrugged. "Dad would have been eighty-six now if he were alive."

"Can I look at them? Maybe read them?" Sage asked.

"Sure," Horace said. "I was thinking of reading it someday to see the world through Dean Aubry's eyes. I was hoping I might have a better handle on who he was because God knows I didn't really know my father growing up, even though we lived in the same house. He avoided me like the plague and gave his attention mostly to Paul. Maybe his writings will help clear up why he only liked his firstborn."

Sage nodded. "I'll handle the journals carefully and return them to you in the same condition."

"Fair enough," Horace said. "But there is no hurry. I barely have time these days to scratch my head. My wife is complaining that I'm too busy."

He stopped at two double-wide doors, that were intricately carved with white and gold trimmings.

"Here is the library," he said, opening the doors.

It was a cozy yet grand room, filled with dark mahogany shelves that reached the high ceiling. Antique rugs covered the floor, and a large unused fireplace stood against one wall, with a portrait of Dean Aubry hanging above it. To both sides of that portrait were two smaller ones. They were of Dean and his wife, Rosa, and their three children—Paul, Donna, and Horace. They were in their Sunday best. The children were probably pre-teens. Horace was obviously younger, the only happy face in the glum painting.

"You guys looked so innocent," Sage breathed. "But even in the family portrait, you looked different—much happier."

Horace laughed. "I don't know why they were so glum. All of them."

"And who is this other family?" Sage asked.

"That's my dad's parents, Benjamin and Iris Aubry," Horace said. "They were an interracial couple. Their marriage was remarkable back in their day. And the children are my dad and his brother, Dale."

Sage moved closer to the portrait. Benjamin was a tall, slim white man with a narrow face, while Iris was a plump, light-skinned woman with a high bouffant hairstyle. Their two sons, Dean and Dale, were a perfect combination of both. Dean, especially the younger of the two, inherited his father's green eyes. With his curly brown hair and pale green eyes, he looked dashing in his individual portrait as an older man. Her father, Paul, resembled him strongly.

"Your grandfather looks like a mixture of both his parents," Bruce said beside her. "And your father resembles your grandfather the most."

Sage inhaled raggedly; she hadn't realized Bruce had moved to stand beside her. "True, I was just thinking the same thing," she whispered.

"Where is Dale?" she asked Horace.

"He is buried in the family plot," Horace replied. "He was part of the Caribbean contingent in World War II. He was an Air Force man. Unfortunately, he died in the war. He got a hero's burial."

"He sounds like he was an incredible man."

"He possibly was," Horace said. "Everyone spoke highly of him, and that in itself is a miracle in this family. Maybe because he died young, he didn't get a chance to create havoc in the community."

Sage chuckled.

Horace went over to a large, antique desk near the center of the room. "This is where my father spent most of his time," he said, patting the back of a well-worn leather chair. "And here are his personal journals."

He opened a drawer and carefully pulled out three old, leather-bound books, placing them gently on the desk. "He had them in his locked drawer," Horace said. "Maybe they hold secrets."

Sage went over and picked up one of the journals. She flipped through the pages; Dean Aubry's handwriting was neat and distinctive, making for easy reading. "I can't wait to dive into them."

Horace smiled. "Take your time. There's no rush. I'm just glad someone will finally read them. And who knows, maybe they'll offer some insights into the man my father was."

Sage nodded, still absorbed in the journal she was holding. "Thank you for trusting me with these, Horace. I'll handle with care."

Horace looked at Bruce, who was looking through the windows at the garden below, his mind racing with ideas. He could go more formal with the driveway and add a bit of whimsy at the sides.

"I see you're contemplating the grounds," Horace said. "It was magnificent during Grandma Iris's time. We had a team of gardeners back in our heyday. My grandmother Iris even gave garden tours."

"I can imagine," Bruce said. "I'm itching to bring it back to its former glory."

Horace nodded. "Iris had the greenest thumb I've ever known. She spent hours out there every day. She famously said she wanted to die in her gardens."

"Do you have any old photos of the gardens?" Sage asked, putting down the journal.

"I do, actually," Horace replied, walking over to a large wooden cabinet. He opened a drawer and pulled out a leather-bound photo album. "These are from the 1950s. The garden was at its peak then."

Sage and Bruce leaned in as Horace opened the album, revealing black-and-white photographs of lush greenery, blooming flowers, and carefully manicured lawns. There were arbors draped in queen's wreath and paths lined with vibrant hibiscus.

"Wow," Sage breathed, her eyes wide with admiration.

"It's stunning."

"It really was," Bruce said. He pointed to a picture where two lignum vitae trees framed the driveway. "It seems you were right, Sage. There were lignum vitae trees here at one time."

Horace nodded. "The trees were there before I was born. A storm uprooted them, I think. For years, there was no tree there, until my father planted a mango tree in one of the lignum vitae slots. He was twenty at the time, a year before he married my mother."

Horace looked as if he wanted to say more but changed his mind.

"That's over fifty years!" Sage said out loud.

"Oh yes," Horace nodded. "Sixty-five years ago, to be exact."

"Mango trees can live for over three hundred years and still bear fruit," Bruce said. "We have a hundred-year-old one on my parents' farm. It's still a trusty bearer."

"One hundred years, interesting," Horace rubbed his chin. "Is it a special variety?"

"No," Bruce said, "just the regular common mango, like the one you have at the front."

"There are stories about the mango tree at the front and why my father planted it," Horace said. "I have never really taken them seriously. Maybe he explains why in his journal, Sage."

Sage nodded. "If I find anything, I'll let you know."

"He was rabidly against anyone cutting down the tree in his lifetime," Horace grimaced. "He didn't exactly help with the speculation surrounding it."

"And what is your take on it being cut down?" Bruce asked. "Because I don't think that tree will fit into the design plans. I'll need to cut it down drastically and spray it for termites."

"Cut it down, uproot it, do whatever it takes to bring the garden back to its former glory," Horace said. "I have many more mango trees around the property that you can save."

Chapter Eight

It was quite a morning at Aubry House. Sage trudged behind the men as they discussed the landscape layout and ideas for the place. She took some drone shots for the before pictures and stood with Horace under the mango tree at the base of the driveway while Bruce explored by himself.

The mysterious mango tree loomed above her, its sparse green foliage casting a dappled shadow.

Horace cleared his throat. "I know you'll hear the story from someone else, so I may as well tell you. Our family has always been the subject of gossip; some stories are true, and some are way out there. I don't know about this one, though. I heard it when I was a boy in high school. My siblings never discussed it, and I would have been afraid to ask my father if it were true."

"Why's that?" Sage asked, intrigued.

"Those sorts of questions would have earned me a thorough spanking," Horace said. "We did not do heart-to-heart talks. We were as formal as you can imagine."

"What is it?" Sage urged him on.

"Oh, the story," Horace said, leaning on the tree trunk. "It's rumored that my father killed a girl from the community and buried her here."

"Which community?" Sage asked disbelievingly.

"The one down the hill—Ben's Valley. If you had taken a left while on the main road, you would have passed through it before you got here. It is named after my great-grandfather, Benjamin Senior. At one point, the Aubrys owned all the land in the valleys; we produced sugar cane. After the abolition of slavery, a huge swathe of land was given to the former slaves."

"Our family… owned slaves?" Sage asked, confused.

"Unfortunately," Horace nodded. "The plantation was on the other side of the hill. It was burnt to the ground in the slave rebellion. That's when they built this one in the late 1800s and started paying people according to the government's dictates."

"So let me get this straight: my great-great-grandfather was a slave owner, my grandfather was a murderer, and my father a pedophile?"

"We don't know if your grandfather was a murderer," Horace said. "That's just speculation. He died twenty years ago. The priest and Donna and I were there—he never confessed anything. He never told us he loved us or was sorry for being such an unpleasant human being. He only said, 'Don't chop down the mango tree.'"

"And you didn't find that suspicious?" Sage asked.

"No, not really," Horace said. "He was attached to this tree. He would come down here to meditate sometimes. I thought nothing of it. I still don't. Unfortunately, the rumor mill has turned the murder story into something of an urban legend around here."

"Who was it?" Sage frowned. "The person he's rumored to have killed?"

"A young woman named Tessa Arlington," Horace sighed. "The story goes that she rejected his advances numerous times, and he became obsessed with her. Then he figured out a way to win her heart. He would pay her school fees—she wanted to become a nurse, and he promised her he would finance it without expecting anything in return."

"And she bought that?" Sage asked.

"According to the story, she did. She got accepted to college and was preparing to go when my father told her to come to the house for the first payment. And that's where the story gets cloudy," Horace sighed. "I've heard two versions of it. One is that he locked her into the library and forced himself on her for a full year until she gave in and became submissive. Then his father forced him to let her go because he had found a bride for him from a suitable family. Upon hearing that, Tessa killed herself. She was ruined and about to be rejected. My father, heartbroken by her actions, buried her in the hole left by the lignum vitae tree and planted a mango tree in its place."

"Ah," Sage nodded. "So what's the other version?"

"The other version is that after he lured her up to the house with promises to pay for her schooling, she resisted him. They fought. He killed her and buried her in the hole left by the lignum vitae tree."

"Both versions are gruesome," Sage shuddered. "Did Tessa Arlington really go missing?"

"She left the community, and no one has heard from her since," Horace said. "But her leaving, combined with my father's obsession with her and the planting of this mango tree, may have been just a coincidence."

"As well as not," Sage said.

"True," Horace sighed. "I guess we'll find out when the tree comes down."

"Or if Tessa shows up here alive and well," Sage murmured.

Horace chuckled. "I doubt that. She won't bother returning now if she hasn't shown up in sixty-six years. People have claimed to see her right under this tree over the years, with her bags packed and crying."

Sage looked around fearfully.

"She only appears at night and only to a discerning eye," Horace chuckled. "Or so the legend says."

Sage laughed with him. "I have to admit, I believe he did it. Your family seems more than a little touched with drama."

Horace smiled. "Believe it or not, we're not all bad in this family."

"Stephen told Cayenne that you and your sons were the only good ones left," Sage said.

"I'll take Stephen's endorsement," Horace shook his head, "but he's not one of the good Aubrys. I heard about that business with Stephen—how he had an elaborate scheme to rob you and your sister of your inheritance."

Sage nodded.

"His father was a crook, too," Horace said. "Sadly, he married Donna because of her inheritance. Donna just blindly handed him her money. I could see him coming a mile away, salivating over her money instead of her."

"I warned her. I really did," Horace continued. "But she was in love. I've found that people stop using logic when they are in love."

Sage chuckled.

"It's true," Horace said. "It's a malady that attacks both

men and women of all ages and stages, so beware."

Sage nodded.

"I'm serious, Sage," Horace continued. "You're a rich woman, whether you like it or not. I know your father made arrangements for you and your sister. It's the Aubry way—we always provide for the next generation."

"Nobody knows I'm rich," Sage said. I doubt I'll be pursued for it, and I like to keep it that way."

Horace nodded. "Good. When I got my share of the inheritance from my father, I started the construction business with it and made some investments here and there. I was a good custodian of the money. You should do the same. Don't let it go to waste. And don't for one minute believe you didn't deserve it. Despite your mother's reservations, you and Cayenne deserve everything and more."

"I've already decided to do something with it," Sage said. "Have you spoken to Paul since he got out?"

"I speak to him often enough," Horace said. "I consider what he has to be more of a disease than anything else. He's implied repeatedly that he got his issues from our father. I saw no evidence of that growing up, but I've heard stories." Horace shrugged. "They are my family. I didn't choose them; they were already chosen for me."

"My mother says that all the time," Sage said.

"She's right," Horace nodded. "If individuals in the family are bad, stay out of their way but keep in touch with the good ones. Speaking of which, you should come over for dinner sometime. I live close to here on the other side of the hill."

Sage nodded. "I'd like that."

"My first wife, Karla, died in a car crash twenty-four years ago. Our two boys were just toddlers and in the car with her, but they escaped without serious injury. I married my second wife, Mindy, fifteen years ago. She's far younger than I am and keeps me on my toes. She would love to meet you. She insists I reach out to you and Cayenne now that you are adults."

"Mindy is family-oriented, which is good because her family is big. She has seven siblings and a whole army of cousins. They are refreshingly normal. I'm sometimes amazed at how run-of-the-mill they are—no thieves, murderers, or criminals."

Sage laughed out loud.

Bruce approached them from the left and stopped to inspect what looked like an old fountain.

Sage watched him helplessly, contemplating whether she should confess her feelings to him. What would his reaction be?

"So, what's the deal with you and Bruce?" Horace asked, watching her watch Bruce.

Sage dragged her eyes from Bruce and shrugged. "He's my boss."

Horace laughed heartily. "You don't look at him as if he's just your boss."

"He's a bit older than me," Sage said.

"Age is nothing but a number," Horace said. "I'm fifteen years older than Mindy. We make it work."

"Okay, all set," Bruce said as he approached them.

"Oh yes," Horace nodded. "I'm really looking forward to the transformation."

Chapter Nine

Bruce had a long conversation with the project manager on one of his sites on the way to his parents' farm. He hung up the phone and looked across at Sage.

"Sorry about that, Sage."

"No problem," Sage said. "I know you have other projects going on."

"Did you have a good talk with Horace?"

"I did," Sage nodded. "I like him. He has a healthy sense of humor and is under no delusions about the type of family he was born into. I think he is one Aubry I wouldn't mind getting to know."

"He has a good reputation in his profession," Bruce said. "Everybody wants to work with Horace Aubry. He is famous for paying at the top end of the spectrum, and because of that, people usually go above and beyond for him. He is good people."

"He told me the story about the mango tree," Sage said. "I

am itching to include it in your docuseries."

"What's the story?" Bruce asked.

"Dean Aubry allegedly buried a woman under the mango tree. Her name was Tessa Arlington."

"Tessa Arlington?" Bruce murmured. "My housekeeper's maiden name is Arlington, and she is from Ben's Valley. I wonder if they are related."

Sage clapped her hands. "Well, if they are, maybe she knows a little more about the story, and we could include it."

"If Horace won't mind," Bruce said. "If it shows his father in a bad light, I am not sure he would want to dredge that up."

Sage nodded. "True. But a story like that could also give exposure to Aubry House. Every house needs a story. It would be good marketing for both of you."

"You have a point," Bruce said. "Maybe you should check Dean Aubry's journals and see if he says anything about it. Maybe he has a confession written in there."

Sage nodded. "I will do that. I can't wait to delve into that today. How long do you think the house project will take?"

"About two to three months," Bruce said. I'll design the plan by the end of this week and then wait for Horace's approval. If he approves it, I'll bring in the guys next week. We'll do the prep work, which includes overhauling that pond feature at the back of the property, turning it into a modern waterfall, and inserting an infinity pool on the terrace area."

"I can't wait to see the transformation," Sage said eagerly. "I envy you, your job. You get to be in the thick of things and experience the joy of transforming an ordinary space into something extraordinary."

"It sounds like you are seriously interested in the nitty-gritty of things," Bruce said.

"I am," Sage said. "It's an obsession of mine. Why do you think I gave Brian my resume to hand to you? I was using the social media manager job as a stepping stone. I want to learn all I can about the landscaping arts."

Bruce looked impressed. "Well, passion like that is hard to come by. If you're serious about this, I'd happily take you under my wing and teach you the ropes. We can start with this project. It'll be a great learning opportunity for you."

Sage's eyes lit up. "Really? That would be amazing, Bruce. I promise I'll work hard and soak up everything I can. I'll ask too many questions and bug you a bit too."

Bruce smiled. "I don't think I'll mind, Sage."

They slowed down at a sign to an entrance that read Whitlock Mango Farms. Before them were rows and rows of mango trees, most about six feet high and loaded with red mangoes.

"Oh wow," Sage breathed. "They look like decorations. I have never in my life seen so many mangoes together. It's beautiful."

Bruce laughed. "Tis the season. My father does these for export. By next week, they will all be gone. They've started picking on the west side of the property already."

He drove up to a gate, and a security guard greeted them.

"We only have security guards during harvesting time," Bruce said.

"How many acres is this?" Sage asked in awe.

As far as the eye could see, there were rows and rows of mangoes.

"It's just twenty-five acres now," Bruce said. "In the past, the operation was much larger, but my father decided to diversify after a bad storm wrecked a good section of the mango trees on the east side of the land. My brother Robert runs the farm now. My dad is retired. He spends his days with his pals golfing. He has turned into a man of leisure after years of hard work."

"Oh," Sage said. "And what does your mother do?"

"She is a retired midwife who still helps deliver babies," Bruce chuckled. "She constantly harangues my brothers to give her grandchildren. Robert is a perpetual bachelor, and Garrick's wife is a career-oriented woman who doesn't have children in her current plans."

"What about you? Doesn't she harass you?" Sage asked.

"No," Bruce smiled. "I gave her Brian, her only grandchild. I am spared for now, but I have promised her that I will eventually, maybe, possibly give her another one or two grandchildren to spoil, so she is fine with that."

Sage chuckled. "Brian will hate not being an only child."

"He'll get used to it and love his siblings," Bruce glanced at her. "So, do you want to have children?"

"I've never really thought about it," Sage said. "My oldest sister had a baby, and he was so cute I got all broody, but after babysitting him for a whole weekend, I have a new respect for parenting. I am still on the fence about motherhood and all it entails."

Bruce nodded. "Quite understandable."

"We are now entering the residential section of the farm," he said, changing the subject. "My parents' place is over there."

They passed a sprawling farmhouse with a gorgeous flower garden in the front.

"Oh wow," Sage said. "That's a pretty garden."

"My first practice spot," Bruce said. "That's where Brian grew up."

"I was supposed to attend your parent's 50th wedding anniversary," Sage said. "Unfortunately, I couldn't make it."

She didn't want to tell him that she decided not to attend after meeting him. Bruce looked across at her as if reading her mind, a knowing look in his eyes.

She dearly hoped he wasn't actually reading her mind, or she would be mortified.

"Whose house is that?" Sage asked as they passed another sprawling farmhouse.

"That's Robert's house," Bruce said. "And beside him is Garrick's house, and beside his is Lionel Henderson's house. He is the foreman."

"They are nice houses," Sage whistled. "You did the gardens too, I bet. They all look gorgeous."

"Guilty," Bruce grinned. "I practiced on all the gardens on this stretch. My family was only too happy to give me free rein."

"This section of the property is supposed to be family accommodation," Bruce said. "It's a U-shaped stretch of land divided into half-acre plots. My dad wanted us to have a Whitlock subdivision where all the family would live in the same spot and work on the farm." Bruce chuckled. "He didn't foresee that we would choose different careers."

"So, where do the workmen stay?" Sage asked.

"They stay in the cabin on the farm section. My father has some cabins over there for the seasonal workers."

"Oh," Sage said.

"We can walk over there one day, but for now, you will be roughing it with me," Bruce grinned.

"Roughing it?" Sage raised her eyebrows.

"I'm just kidding," Bruce said as he slowed down before a modern farmhouse. It was a single-story house with a wraparound porch, large windows, and a beautifully landscaped front yard. The exterior was painted a warm, inviting shade of cream, with dark green shutters adding a touch of contrast. Flower beds brimming with colorful blooms lined the path to the front door.

"This is it," Bruce said, parking the truck and turning off the engine. "Welcome to my humble abode."

Sage took in the sight, feeling a mixture of relief and excitement. "It's beautiful, Bruce. Not exactly roughing it."

Bruce laughed. "Yeah, I might have exaggerated a bit. We have Wi-Fi out here, but fair warning, it is temperamental, especially when it rains. If you need to do anything internet-related and the Wi-Fi starts acting up, we use Garrick's office in town. He is usually a gracious host."

"When Brian said he grew up on a farm, I wasn't expecting this," Sage said, looking around. "The house is nice, but the gardens are even nicer. I can tell this is a landscape designer's place."

"Thank you," Bruce said. "I was going for simple yet functional. I do the garden work myself when I am out here."

"And you don't like the yellow," Sage said. "I see purples and whites and a dash of reds. Is that a tropical hibiscus? Why is the bloom so huge?"

She went closer to the plant.

"It is tropical," Bruce nodded. "I've been experimenting with breeding different varieties to create larger blooms. It's a hobby of mine. I try creating unique hybrids you don't usually see around here."

Sage examined the hibiscus closely, admiring the intricate details of the petals. "It's stunning. You have quite the talent, Bruce."

Bruce smiled modestly. "Thank you. It's a labor of love. Gardening is my way of relaxing and connecting with nature. And yes, you are very observant—I tend to stay away from yellow for my personal garden designs, but I have no problem yellowing it up for clients. I take it you like yellows?"

"I love it," Sage said. "It makes me feel happy. I have this vision of a garden with bright yellow and contrasting purple."

"Mmm," Bruce said. "I've done one of those before."

They entered the farmhouse through a giant front door. The interior was airy and light.

"I feel like clapping," Sage said. "I love this."

Bruce grinned. "Clap away. I wish I could take credit for the design, but Garrick's wife, Amber, designed it. She usually does commercial spaces, but she said she would have a go at this for me, and this is the result."

"Gorgeous!" Sage said. And it was. It was an open-plan living room with high ceilings and exposed wooden beams. Large windows allowed natural light to flood in, and a giant potted tree occupied one corner, surrounded by plush sofas and armchairs. The kitchen was seamlessly integrated into the living area; an island with bar stools provided a perfect spot for casual meals or conversations, and there was a perfect little nook in the kitchen overlooking a herb garden and, beyond that, a lake. It was picturesque.

"This is the perfect place for a family," Sage murmured. "It's amazing."

"It really is," a stout lady with a husky voice said as she entered through the side door. "I sit outside in the guest house and thank my lucky stars I work in such a location. I have all the mangoes I can eat and a view that looks like it was dredged from a children's storybook."

Bruce chuckled. "Sage, meet Blossom Arlington McKenzie, my housekeeper. Her husband, Simon, is one of my project managers. They live in the guest house at the back."

Blossom smiled widely. "Hello, Miss Aubry."

"How do you know my surname?" Sage asked, confused. "Bruce didn't say."

"You look like them," Blossom said. "I'm from Ben's Valley."

"Oh," Sage chuckled. "I thought the family was small."

"The legitimate part," Blossom chuckled. "But there are several outside children who are clearly Aubry and living in Ben's Valley."

Bruce cleared his throat. "Blossom, try not to overwhelm Sage with your folklore just yet. Give her some time to settle in. I'm going to get the bags from the car."

"I'll show her around," Blossom said helpfully.

"Thank you," Bruce nodded.

"Now, Miss," Blossom said, looking around. "This is the living room and kitchen area. Mr. Bruce's section is to the left—his office and the primary suite are over there."

She led Sage to Bruce's section, which was decorated the same way as the rest of the house, except that his room had dark blue and gray accents.

"It looked like him," Sage thought, and it smelled like him too. A portrait of Bruce, Brian, and a girl in pigtails sat on the living room table. Brian and the girl, who looked about ten, were hugging Bruce around his neck and grinning at the camera. Sage understood why he would frame it; it was a happy picture.

"That's Brian, his son," Miss Blossom said behind her. "And the little girl with them is Natalia. She's Luke Henderson's daughter. Henderson has lived here for most of his life; it's no wonder Brian and Natalia grew up together."

"Oh," Sage said, looking closer at the picture; Brian was a cute, chubby version of himself now, with his overly long curls and mischievous smile. "I went to university with Brian."

She hesitated to mention that she had dated him for eighteen months. Why on earth was she so touchy about that, anyway? She knew about Natalia because Brian talked about her a lot. He didn't have a story without Natalia featuring prominently in it.

"Brian has grown into a lovely young man," Blossom said proudly. "I like to think I had a hand in that. I babysat him and Natalia when they were younger—a rambunctious pair, those two. And I was happy to see it when they got older and started dating."

"But look how life turned out," Blossom shook her head. "They didn't end up together, and now Natalia is supposedly engaged to Shane Magnus. Poor Brian is heartbroken. When he came here a few months ago, he was devastated."

Sage was a little stunned. Natalia was getting married? Brian was devastated? Obviously, Blossom didn't know she was even a feature in their lives.

Good. She wasn't jealous about Brian or Natalia, just feeling a little put out that she had dated Brian for eighteen months and hadn't known that theirs had been some sort of rebound relationship. No wonder she had always felt as if something was missing.

She followed Blossom around the house as she showed her Bruce's office, the two guest rooms, and the en-suite bathrooms. Bruce had already placed her bags in the back guest room; it had a patio with a view of the lake through the trees.

He paced back and forth on the patio as he talked to someone about one of his job. When they entered the room, he hung up the phone and looked up at her and Blossom apologetically.

"I'm going to have to go to Montego Bay," he said. "There's a little glitch on a work site. I'll be back tonight.

Save me dinner."

"I hope you enjoy your stay here, Sage," he continued. You can work in my office if you want."

And just like that, he was gone.

Sage looked after him with a helpless longing.

"Don't worry, dearie," Blossom said breezily. "He'll be back soon. In the meantime, do you want a light or heavy lunch?"

"I can do without him for a while," Sage protested. "We are just work colleagues."

Blossom chuckled. "Of course, dear."

Chapter Ten

Bruce came in way too late for dinner. Sage had already gone to bed. The house was quiet, and Miss Blossom had put his plate in the fridge. It was well-covered and ready to be microwaved.

He put the plate in the microwave and watched as it went round and round. He wasn't feeling as tired as he initially had when leaving the work site in Montego Bay. His project manager had panicked when the customer decided to change a significant part of the agreed-upon plan. He had to personally sort that out. Feathers were ruffled, but all was now well on that work site.

He hadn't had time to think about Sage, even on his way back, as he had other business matters to deal with.

He glanced at the clock; it was just after ten. The microwave beeped, and his phone rang at the same time. It was Brian.

"What's up, Dad?"

"I just got in from Montego Bay and am about to eat,"

Bruce said, opening his plate and looking at his brown stew fish, mashed potatoes, and vegetable medley. Nobody cooked fish like Miss Blossom. It smelled heavenly. He inhaled deeply. "What's up with you?"

"Counting down the days till I get home," Brian said. "I have six weeks to go. Exams are hard but manageable."

"Good," Bruce said. "I'm going to put you on speakerphone. Pardon me if I'm not coherent; I'm about to consume Miss Blossom's fish."

"You're in St. Ann!" Brian said.

"Yes, I am," Bruce said. "I told you this already."

"I completely forgot," Brian muttered. "Do you know what Sage is up to? She's not answering her phone."

"She's here in St. Ann with me," Bruce said. "We're doing a docuseries for social media. When I got in, she was already in bed."

"Wait a minute," Brian yelped. "You mean she's staying with you?"

"Yes," Bruce started eating. "What's the problem?"

"That means she's going to meet Natalia without me there," Brian fretted. "I can't have that."

Bruce chuckled. "Not interested in your little drama."

"Has she said anything about me?" Brian asked. "She's been giving me the cold shoulder lately."

"I don't want to get involved in your love life," Bruce said honestly. It was bad enough that he was attracted to Sage. Gossiping about her with Brian was beyond the pale. He had left the 'she loves me, she loves me not' drama in college.

"She said something," Brian said. "And it wasn't complimentary."

"Why would you say that?" Bruce asked.

"Because if it had been complimentary, you would have

readily said something," Brian sighed. "Why do I feel like I'm on the losing end of this? Natalia is getting married to Shane, and Sage is trying to break up with me. What's wrong with me, Dad?"

"Absolutely nothing," Bruce said. "You are a wonderful young man—handsome, intelligent, caring, kind. I could go on and on with the accolades."

"But the two girls I'm interested in are not interested in me," Brian moaned. "Maybe I'm too strait-laced and proper. I should have dropped out of school at fifteen, drank, smoked, wore my pants almost to my ankles, talked like I had a speech impediment, and slept with every girl who would have me in the neighborhood."

Bruce hooted with laughter. "Son, you are fine just the way you are. You just described Shane to a T, though. Please tell me you're not jealous of him."

"I am," Brian said. "How could Natalia even think of marrying him? Most of the time, he isn't even clean."

"He's a mechanic," Bruce said. "That's to be expected. He's probably the best mechanic in Jamaica. That man is a genius with vehicles, and his shop is swamped with high-end vehicles that only he can fix. And he might not be able to string two sentences together, but have you heard him sing? I think if he really tried to do it professionally, he'd succeed at that too. There's something to be admired about a kid who dropped out of high school but started his own business at sixteen and is making a success of it."

"Dad, whose side are you on here?" Brian asked exasperatedly.

"Always yours," Bruce said. "But I must say, I don't think you should be so distressed over Shane. Natalia is not your girlfriend anymore; she has moved on, and so have you. Remember?"

Brian was silent. "What are my chances if I ask Sage to marry me now? What do you think?"

"So we're back to Sage," Bruce sighed. "And you want to marry her because Natalia and Shane are getting married?"

"Yes," Brian said. "Do you think she will outright say no?"

"Yes," Bruce said. "She said she was in love with someone else. Besides, I would strongly discourage you from even thinking of using her that way."

"I'm going to ask her," Brian said. "Maybe she'll say yes."

"Oh dear," Bruce murmured. "You're in that zone where you're not listening to a word I have to say. I just told you that Sage is in love with someone else, and your first instinct is to ask her to marry you?"

"I'll call her tomorrow," Brian said. "We'll set things straight. Night, Dad."

"Night, Brian," Bruce hung up the phone and looked at it ruefully. He had gone through his young and confused stage once. Time had a way of sorting out complex relationship issues.

And he was patiently waiting for time to solve his inexplicably intense attraction to Sage. An attraction that had burrowed itself so deep under his skin that he was beginning to think of it as something more. What if he loved her?

What if this tender, prolonged feeling toward Sage was love?

Then he'd be in real trouble. And he needed to nip it in the bud quickly. But he had been trying—how does one stop feelings of love? He had no clue. The honest truth was he had never felt this way about anyone. He was in serious trouble.

****

He had spent most of the night after dinner reviewing the old diagrams of Aubrey house. He decided to make some improvements to the design. The gardens had been spectacular before, and there was no need to reinvent the wheel in several areas of the three-acre property. It would once again be a showpiece when he was done.

He started plugging the diagram into his design software to get a realistic rendition of what to expect, but weariness overtook him. He showered and hit the bed by midnight but was up by four, working steadily to input all the information when Sage walked into the kitchen around seven. She was dressed in track bottoms that swamped her, but still looked adorable. Her hair was piled on her head in disarray, and she headed straight for the coffee pot.

"Good morning," he said.

She jumped. "Good morning."

"What's on the itinerary for today?" Bruce asked.

Sage rubbed her eyes and blinked at him. "I'll follow your lead. We can have a little discussion about the plan and what you intend to do. You can explain your process. I'll include some live shots of where you plan to make changes. That could be our episode one."

"I'm almost done with the design," Bruce said.

"That was fast," Sage widened her eyes. "I thought you'd be holed up in your office for the rest of the week working on it."

"Well, usually that might be the case, but the former pictures of the place were helpful, and the software makes it easier. Back in the day, when you were a toddler, I had to do it by hand. It would take me weeks then, but now the process is much quicker."

"Oh, wow," Sage chuckled. "Tell me more about the olden days of the early 2000s. Did you guys have electricity?"

Bruce grinned. "We did."

"And electric appliances?" Sage raised an eyebrow.

"Okay," Bruce said. "I may have laid it on a bit thick, but you're way younger than I am."

"You're not that old, Bruce," Sage said.

"When you were three, I was graduating college," Bruce said. "My son is the same age as you are."

"Why are we comparing ages again?" Sage asked.

"I just thought I'd take the opportunity to point out that we're from different generations," Bruce said. "It helps me keep things in perspective, reminding myself that you could be my daughter."

Sage raised an eyebrow. "Age and maturity are two different things. Some older people are immature, and some younger people are quite wise."

Bruce smiled. "I know that. Tell me, what do you do for fun? What are your likes and dislikes?"

"For fun," Sage said, "I like to watch gardening shows, read, go to the movies, attend concerts, hang out with my sisters or friends, play the violin, and travel. I like pineapple-flavored things, prefer cats to kittens, and I dislike discussing religion and politics. With those two subjects, everyone is an expert, and their ways are always right while mine are wrong. So, I don't bother."

"And what do you look for in a partner?" Bruce asked. "What made you fall in love with the guy you are in love with now?"

"Ahm," Sage stuttered. "I… I don't want to talk about it."

"Come on," Bruce said, "why not?"

"It's unrequited," Sage said, blushing. "I am totally embarrassed about it."

"Oh, and why is that?" Bruce asked, leaning in with interest.

"Just because," Sage shrugged.

Bruce changed the subject abruptly. "Did you get a chance to run through your grandfather's journals? Anything of interest?"

"I haven't started reading it," Sage said. "I was out like a light as soon as my head hit the pillow. I like it here."

"You can stay as long as you want," Bruce said, trying to keep his voice neutral. "You don't have to leave for the weekend."

"That would be great," Sage nodded. "But I have to return to Kingston for my sister's dress fitting and to update my wardrobe. Otherwise, I would totally take you up on the offer. I slept like a baby last night."

"That's how it was for most of my childhood," Bruce said. "We worked on the farm, and when we came home, we were so drained that we were out like a light."

He opened his laptop again. "I am going to show Horace these plans today and see what he says. If I have to make changes, I will, and then we can start filming."

"Cool," Sage nodded. "Too bad you're going back to work. I didn't get to ask about your likes and dislikes and what you look for in a partner."

Bruce chuckled. "I am as simple and basic as they come. My hobby is my business, so I am totally consumed by it. Most of the things I like are garden and landscape related. I like visiting flower shows from around the world, experimenting with creating new species of hibiscus, and I enjoy 90s R&B. I don't mind a Netflix and chill as a perfect date, or camping under the stars. I dislike selfishness in all its forms, especially in a relationship."

"Would you date a woman younger than you?" Sage asked.

"How young are you talking?" Bruce replied.

"Say Brian's age," Sage shrugged.

Bruce looked at her for way longer than he should before finally saying, "I may make an exception if the person is special and we have a deep connection. She'd have to be exceptional, though. I hear age-gap romances are more trouble than they're worth. And if she's twenty-one, she's just starting life, feeling herself around the relationship maze. It would be wrong to tie her down in a committed relationship at that stage. I don't want to be an albatross around her neck, a mistake she'll regret when she gets older."

"Why would you assume that a woman of twenty-one wouldn't know her mind?" Sage frowned.

"Because people grow and change. I was not the person I was even ten years ago. My priorities are certainly different from when I was twenty-nine. Right now, I date with purpose. I'm thinking of a long-term commitment and children."

"Some twenty-one-year-olds want that," Sage said.

"Do you?" Bruce asked skeptically.

"I don't know," Sage said, putting her cup on the counter. "But I'm not twenty-one; I'm twenty-two. And as you said, the guy has to be special if he's older."

Bruce chuckled. "Sage, take your time in life, enjoy your twenties, and say no to whatever marriage proposals you get today."

Sage laughed. "If the proposal comes from my secret love, I won't say no."

Bruce sighed, frustrated by her secret love, whoever he was. "I'm going to take this to the office."

He got up abruptly and took his laptop. The thought occurred to him that he was acting erratically, so he slowed down and turned around to apologize. But Sage was staring at him with so much emotion he couldn't ignore it.

Her eyes were wide and glistening, filled with a depth of feeling that took him aback. It was as if a veil had lifted, and he could finally see the truth that had been in front of him all along. He was the man she was in love with.

He had several options: admit he felt the same or ignore it.

He chose to ignore it.

"I'm sorry to leave so abruptly," he murmured. "I have a ton of things to finish."

"I understand," Sage nodded. "Please do not let me interrupt your flow."

He nodded and then headed to the office with much less steam than he had initially felt. He had a lot to think about.

Chapter Eleven

After Bruce left for his office, Sage ran the conversation through her mind, turning and twisting it as she tried to make sense of it.

Sage replayed every word in her head, dissecting Bruce's tone and expressions. Had he asked her about dating someone older because he was interested in her? His reaction to her secret love had been particularly telling—could it be that he was jealous?

Maybe he saw her in a different light. Maybe he actually liked her?

The idea made her heart flutter, but she quickly dismissed it. It was too risky to entertain such thoughts without more clarity.

And what proposal was he telling her to reject?

Who was going to propose? What did he know?

Was his advice about not accepting a way to keep her from getting hurt, or was it a subtle hint that he might feel something for her?

The questions were driving her crazy. She finally gave up on trying to decipher the conversation with Bruce and went for her grandfather's journals; it would be a welcome distraction.

Hopefully, she would find something on the mango tree mystery and get an insight into who Dean Aubry was.

She opened the first journal. He numbered his entries and had a smooth writing style that was engaging and easy to read.

Journal Entry #1-July 10, 1985

I am fifty years old when I started these journals. I am writing them to make sense of my life and to pour out my sorrows, triumphs, and joys, though paltry they are.

If you are reading this, then I am dead. I would be mortified if you read it while I was alive. My life story took a turn for the worse, and I would be uncomfortable exposing my many secrets while I am living.

I also anticipate that if you are reading this, you are a family member. Maybe a grandchild or great-grandchild. I shudder to think that these journals will end up in the hands of strangers.

Even though strangers can sometimes be more empathetic than family, this is my life laid bare.

My name is Dean Benjamin Aubry, I was born on July 10, 1935, a miracle baby. My parents, Benjamin Aubry and Iris Aubry, already had a thirteen-year-old son, Dale, their pride and joy. My mother had several miscarriages before I was born and had all but given up hope that she would have another. Despite my status as a miracle child, I never quite felt like my mother liked me much. My father was a product of his time, not given to outward affection. I often felt lonely in my household. My older brother was off to boarding school when I was a toddler.

I grew up feeling isolated. My only solace was in the various tomes in my father's library. I finally made friends when I sneaked off our hill to the community below. I realized why my mother did not want me to mix with the other children. It wasn't because we were the rich Aubrys, the ones who owned the major source of income for the people down below. No, it was the fact that there were children there who looked a lot like me.

Either my father or grandfather had dalliances with the women in the village because there were many fair-skinned, green-eyed children in Ben's Valley, a town named after my grandfather, the original Benjamin Aubry.

When I went to the valley, I made friends easily. I was especially close to Lionel Vicker and Bradley Benson, and being friends with them marked the beginning of my adventurous childhood.

****

Sage was intrigued. She read further into the journal; Dean Aubry's life as a boy was fascinating. She was on entry number five, where he talked about his various adventures with his friends Lionel and Bradley when Blossom walked in and bid her a cheery good morning.

"Do you want anything to eat, Miss Sage?"

"No thanks," Sage said. "I am not really a breakfast fan."

Blossom grunted. "A hearty breakfast is the building block to the start of a good day."

Sage chuckled and continued reading the journal. She vaguely heard Blossom as she flitted in and out of the kitchen. Then she hit the jackpot: Dean started writing about his late teenage years.

Journal Entry # 20

I met Tessa Arlington two days before my eighteenth birthday. She was walking out of the haberdashery store in a sky-blue dress and white shoes. Her hair was in the popular bouffant hairstyle of the day, with a matching white band and a flower at the side. I felt as if I was struck by lightning. It was swift, immediate, and so life-altering that I literally felt as if I would not be the same again.

Unfortunately, she looked right through me. I am not used to that reaction from the girls in the village. Usually, I am feted and fawned over when I visit Ben's Valley. I am my father's heir since my brother died in World War 2. I am also their future landlord. And not to brag, but I am a handsome fellow. I was born with the best features of both my parents. I have my mother's smile and my father's eyes. I have the phenotype that the girls in the village go crazy for. I have unashamedly sampled more of their charms than I probably should. I have been especially partial to the younger ones. My father has warned me time and again to exercise control, but I have never wanted to until now. I want to be faithful and committed to Tessa Arlington. I want to throw down my coat and let her walk over it. I want to be the air she breathes. I am obsessed. My need for her is like a fire in my veins.

She will love me like I love her.

****

"**W**ould you like some sandwiches and a slice of mango

cake?"

Sage jumped; that last part of the journal entry had been intense. She looked at Blossom, confused.

"You said something, Blossom?"

"I asked, since you didn't eat breakfast, would you like lunch?" Blossom asked patiently.

"Yes, I would love lunch," Sage nodded. "I didn't realize that I was so hungry. I was so caught up in Dean Aubry's journal."

"That murderer," Blossom sniffed.

"What do you know?" Sage asked curiously. "He just mentioned Tessa Arlington. You two have the same last name."

"She was my aunt," Blossom said. "Let me go and get the food, and then we'll chat about your grandfather and what he did to my aunt."

Sage nodded eagerly.

Blossom carried over the food: precision-cut roast beef sandwiches, a yellow-looking cake coated with buttercream frosting, and a pitcher filled with drinks.

"These are pure pineapple drinks," Blossom said. "No sugar added. Mr. Bruce said you love pineapples."

Sage widened her eyes. "I just told him that this morning."

"Well, he took note," Blossom said, sitting down across from Sage. "A man like Mr. Bruce is attentive like that. When some lucky woman finally gets him tied down, she will be well-loved. He reminds me quite a bit of my Simon. When they love, they love hard."

Sage smiled. "It's always nice to be loved."

"Nice is too mild," Blossom said. "It is beautiful. Many people will not experience that in their lifetime."

Sage took a bite of her sandwich and widened her eyes. "This is good, Blossom."

"Thank you," Blossom grinned. "When Mr. Bruce is here, I go all out. I cook everything with love and a dash of hope and dreams that he fills up this place with a family. He is too young to be alone."

Sage chuckled. "Tell me about Tessa Arlington and Dean Aubry."

"My aunt Tessa did not like Dean Aubry," Blossom began. "She was not in the market for a relationship. Back in the forties, she had the lofty idea of being a nurse and not being tied up with marriage and children. She wanted to be an independent woman. It was not a popular idea in those days—even my mother said she did not understand it."

"In the 1940s, women were more commonly expected to focus on homemaking and raising families rather than pursuing careers. Aunt Tessa, however, was determined to carve out a different path for herself. She was headstrong and passionate about her dreams."

Blossom continued, "Dean Aubry, on the other hand, was quite traditionalist. He believed in the conventional roles of men and women, and he couldn't fathom why a woman would want anything different. He was persistent, though, trying to woo Tessa despite her clear disinterest."

"And then what happened?" Sage asked eagerly.

"He was so obsessed," Blossom continued, "he hatched a plan to get her interested in him. He told her he would pay for her schooling if she passed her exams. Aunt Tessa was exuberant. The family couldn't afford to send her to school; she had been operating on hopes and dreams up to that point. So, when she passed her exams, she told Dean Aubry, and he said, 'Come up to the house, and I'll cut you a check.' It was supposed to be a simple transaction. He had told her he expected nothing in return."

Blossom paused, then added, "She went up to the house

that June night in 1944 and never came back home."

"What?" Sage said, shocked. When Horace had told her, she had thought it was an urban legend, a tale, a conspiracy. Hearing this from Tessa Arlington's niece was a shocker.

Blossom nodded. "She never came back. She disappeared off the face of the earth. My grandparents reported it to the police at the time." Blossom grimaced. "But you must understand that accusations against an Aubry would fall on deaf ears. Those people could and have gotten away with murder. They were untouchable. And so we mourned our relative. Year after year, we expected her to come home. She never did."

"Oh no," Sage whispered.

"And then, Beryl Davis saw her," Blossom said.

"She did?" Sage asked.

"Oh yes, Miss Beryl saw things that nobody else could see. She could see into the spirit realm."

"Oh," Sage said, deflated. "Let me guess, she saw her at the mango tree at the bottom of the hill where the house was."

"Yes," Blossom nodded.

"So that's where the story started," Sage said. "I should read the rest of the journals and find out what happened."

"And do you believe Dean Aubry would be truthful?" Blossom raised her eyebrows.

"He did say he would be writing journals to pour out his regrets and sorrows," Sage said. "Maybe killing Tessa was a regret."

Blossom nodded. "Well then, read on and let me know what that man did."

Chapter Twelve

Sage scanned the journals, speed-reading the entries, stopping at every mention of Tessa. She was desperate to find out what happened. Somehow, after reading the few entries from Dean, she had felt a kind of kinship to him. He had come across as sympathetic. It was weird that she anxiously didn't want him to commit murder.

Journal Entry #25

Today, I find myself ensnared in a web of my own making, a trap holding me tightly in its grasp. The events of the day unfolded with a grotesque finality, leaving me with a burden I fear I shall carry to my grave.

I invited Tessa Arlington to Aubry House under the guise of offering financial assistance for her schooling. A check, a simple piece of paper promising her a future free from worry, was the bait. I knew she would come; she always prioritized her education. My intentions, however, were far from altruistic.

When she arrived, her eyes lit up with hope and gratitude as she entered the drawing room. I handed her the check, watching as relief washed over her features. Then, I seized the moment, my heart pounding with the urgency of unspoken words. I declared my feelings for her, every syllable a confession of the love that had consumed me for months. I poured out my heart, laying bare my soul before her.

But Tessa's reaction was not what I had hoped for. Her eyes widened in shock, then narrowed with discomfort. She took a step back, shaking her head. She rejected me, her words slicing through my chest like a dagger. 'I couldn't accept it.' Desperation clawed at me, and I found myself begging her to reconsider, to give us a chance.

Tessa's fear grew palpable. She turned and fled the room, her footsteps echoing in the empty hall. I followed, my pleas falling on deaf ears. Then, it happened. In her haste, she tripped over the edge of the rug and fell. The sound of her head striking the edge of the desk is a noise I will never forget. I rushed to her side, but it was too late. Her lifeless body lay before me, a silent testament to the horror of what had transpired.

Panic gripped me as I called for my father. He arrived swiftly from upstairs, assessing the situation with a cold, calculating gaze. His verdict was swift and uncompromising: we had to conceal what had happened. He instructed me to bury Tessa in the hole left by the lignum vitae trees in the front garden and to speak of this to no one.

I followed his orders mechanically, the weight of my actions pressing down on me with every shovelful of earth. I saw a mango seedling in the bushes and placed it in the center, where I laid her to rest.

The mango tree will stand as a grave marker, a silent witness to the darkness that has taken root in my soul.

What have I done?

I am left with guilt and a hollow ache that will never fade.

I must carry this secret, live with this guilt, and hope that one day, it won't consume me entirely.

****

Sage was stunned after reading the entry. She was still sitting, staring into space, when Bruce emerged from his office.

"Sage, are you okay?"

"Yes, I think so," Sage said. "I don't know what to make of what I just read."

"Did he kill her?" Blossom came into the kitchen.

"No," Sage said. "It's complicated."

"Well, how complicated can it be?" Blossom asked.

"He says he was pursuing her, and she fell, hit her head, and died. His father told him to bury her and not say a word."

"The animals, both of them," Blossom breathed. "That's even more cruel than him leaving us in limbo for all these years. I will tell my mother; she'll be happy to get closure. She'll be eighty this year. Can you imagine it took her sixty-odd years to finally find out the truth about her sister? Sixty-odd years!"

"It's tragic," Bruce stretched and rubbed the back of his neck. "So the legend was true?"

"Seems so," Sage nodded. "I can't imagine what your family went through, Blossom, or why Dean's father would tell him not to say a word."

"Because they didn't think we were humans and had

feelings," Blossom said. "You have no idea how terrible the classism was then. Maybe even a hint of racism too. He probably hated the fact that his son loved a black girl. Maybe he couldn't wait to get rid of her even though she didn't want him."

"But Benjamin Aubry married a black woman!" Sage protested.

"Who was light, bright, and could pass for white," Blossom said. "My aunt Tessa was too dark for marriage. To have her as a plaything would have been fine. After all, most of the Aubry men played with the women down in Ben's Valley indiscriminately, no matter their hue, the hypocrites. We were good enough to be stopgaps until they could find someone more to their class and race. You Aubrys..."

"Don't take it out on me, Blossom. I am just learning about this side of my family. I would prefer not to be lumped with them; thank you very much."

"Sorry," Blossom murmured.

"Let's take a walk," Bruce said to Sage, "and give Blossom a chance to grieve. We both need a break."

"It's going to rain," Blossom warned them. "Dinner should be ready and on the stove when you get back. I am going to choir practice. I hope it holds up until I get back."

Sage got up and stretched. "I can't believe how fast the time slipped by while I was reading."

They headed towards the back door.

"How do you feel about walking in the rain?" Bruce asked.

"It sounds great," Sage said. "As long as there is no lightning, I am good."

Bruce nodded. "My thoughts too. I'll get two raincoats. How are your shoes for walking?"

"My Crocs are fine," Sage said. "They are comfy. I've worn them at a beach before."

"I am going to get my water boots," Bruce said. "We'll stick to the pathways."

"This is sort of romantic," Sage laughed while they trudged in the steady drizzle. "It reminds me of the song, 'Walking in the Rain with the One I Love Feels So Fine'... though I am not implying that this is a romance or anything."

Bruce chuckled, shaking his head. "No worries, Sage. I know we are just two friends braving the elements. At least I hope we are friends."

"Yes, of course," Sage said, looking at him and then away guiltily. She was not thinking about just a friendship with him.

They continued walking, their boots splashing through puddles as the rain pattered gently around them. The only sound they heard was the rhythmic drumming of raindrops on their coats.

"It's peaceful, isn't it?" Sage mused, glancing up at the gray sky. "Almost like the world slows down when it rains."

Bruce nodded, his gaze focused on the path ahead. "Yeah, it's like a different kind of beauty. Sometimes, you just need to take a step back and appreciate it. This used to be one of my favorite pastimes when I'm alone. I'd walk in the rain, and just like that, my thoughts would be clearer, and I'd figure out whatever problem was plaguing me."

"You had a problem?" Sage asked.

"I have a problem," Bruce said. "It's personal. But on the business front, I finally have the designs ready. I also have alternatives. I will present the designs to Horace tomorrow and see what he says."

Sage nodded. "Can I tag along? I want him to know about Tessa Arlington. I'd also like to include a little customer interview for the first episode."

"Sure," Bruce nodded. "That was unfortunate, wasn't it?

The whole business with Tessa?"

"Yep," Sage said, holding her hands to capture the rain as it came down harder. "I wish Dean had said something and given the Arlington family closure."

"Maybe that's why he wrote the journals," Bruce said. "It's too bad that it's over half a century later, but I guess it's better late than never."

Sage nodded contemplatively.

They walked to the end of the driveway, passing all the houses until they reached the farm's entrance.

"We have walked a mile and a half," Bruce said. "When we get back, that'll be three miles. Not bad for a rainy evening stroll, is it?"

"Not bad at all," Sage murmured. "It was a nice break from the heaviness of Dean Aubry's journals. I just read one; two more to go. I wonder if there are any more revelations in the last two."

"But of course," Bruce said, "people born in that era and even before are much more interesting than people in our time. It's just that they didn't have social media or so many news outlets recording their scandalous deeds."

Sage chuckled. "My great-grandmother Saidie always says that. She thinks we are tame compared to back in her days. She has always said that whatever shenanigans we get up to now, they did the same in her days; it was just that it wasn't broadcast as it is now."

"True," Bruce nodded. "The things my grandfather used to do were eyebrow raising."

"Like what?" Sage asked.

"He was a sailor and had a girl in every port," Bruce said. "He was a serial cheater on my poor grandma. He cheated on her till the day he died."

"Wow, that's intense," Sage said, shaking her head. "Your

grandma must have been a strong woman to put up with all that."

"She was," Bruce replied, a hint of admiration in his voice. "She held the family together through it all. She had this quiet strength that I've always admired, but she was perpetually unhappy. His randy ways sucked the life out of her."

"I don't know how some women do it," Sage said. "I may forgive one affair, but two? Nope, not going to happen."

"I agree," Bruce nodded. "Cheating hurts. I say if you can't keep your commitment, leave. Break it off, divorce, sever the connection, and start fresh. That goes for both sexes. Men are not the only ones who cheat."

"I know," Sage nodded. "My mom was born out of a cheating situation, and then it spiraled downhill from there."

"Yes, I remember the frenzied speculation last year when everyone assumed she was Greystone's mistress," Bruce chuckled. "To be honest, I never could picture your mother and Greystone being a couple. I was one of the people who thought he was her father or something."

"Because of the age gap," Sage looked at him curiously. "What age gap do you see working?"

"I think it depends more on the individuals and their connection than their ages," Bruce replied thoughtfully. I've seen couples with significant age gaps who are incredibly happy because they share the same values, interests, and respect for each other, and people who have no age gap divorcing or breaking up. I think it's all relative."

Sage nodded, considering his words. "Yeah, you're right. It's all about the people involved and how they handle their relationship."

Bruce stopped walking and turned to her. "Exactly. The most important thing is mutual respect and understanding.

Age can be just a number if both parties are on the same wavelength."

Sage stopped too. "You know, that's a good way to look at it. My mom always said it's not about finding the perfect person but finding someone who makes you want to be your best self."

The rain came down harder, running in rivulets down their faces as they stared at each other.

"I think I just solved my personal problem," Bruce said huskily. "Thank you."

"You are welcome," Sage swallowed. "Although I am not sure what I did."

"You are as wise as your name suggests; trust me on that," Bruce paused. "About that guy you are in love with..."

Sage inhaled. "I am not going to tell you who it is."

"That's fine," Bruce said. "Don't say anything about your feelings or start something with him until you make a good, clean break with Brian, okay?"

Sage nodded. "Okay."

"If he is worthy, he'll be patient and wait for you," Bruce said. "Besides, you don't want to start another relationship with unresolved baggage. It wouldn't be fair to either of you."

They stood silently for a moment, the rain falling around them. The weight of their conversation lingered in the air.

Did he know that he was the one she was in love with? Was he telling her not to tell him until she was completely free of Brian? All those thoughts ran through her mind while they stared at each other.

What on earth was he thinking?

Finally, Bruce broke the silence. "We should probably get out of this rain. That little walk really worked up an appetite."

Sage nodded. "Yeah, good idea. I am starving as well."

Chapter Thirteen

They got out of the rain just before it turned into a deluge. Despite the raincoat, Sage's pant legs were soaked through, and her hair was damp on one side.

"The electricity is out," Bruce said, flipping the switch when they entered the mudroom. "Don't worry, I have some electric candles."

"I can see well enough," Sage said, her lips trembling. "I am going to have a shower."

"Me too," Bruce said. "Then we'll have dinner, and maybe you can read some of your grandfather's diary to me. After journal one, I am sure journal two is even spicier."

Sage laughed. "I hope not."

She was just about to step into the shower when Brian called.

"Hey."

"Hey," Sage said, her voice flat.

"You could sound happier to hear from me," Brian

accused.

"I am shivering," Sage said, "just about to step into the shower."

"Why are you shivering?" Brian asked.

"I was walking in the rain," Sage said. "It was lovely, but I got wet. Can we talk another time?"

"Wait," Brian said. "I wanted to ask you something."

"What?" Sage put him on speaker and stepped into the shower.

"I know you are staying with my dad," Brian said, "which means you are in the same vicinity as Natalia. I sort of told her that you and I were getting married. Could you back me up on that?"

"No," Sage gasped. "I am not going to lie for you, Brian. What's up with you and Natalia? Why do you always have to one-up her?"

She let the water run over her, trying to calm her growing frustration with Brian. She felt like she was in high school again, playing the little dramas that usually came with early teenage relationships.

"Come on, Sage," Brian persisted. "It's just a small favor. She is planning her wedding to Shane; that's all she talks about, and I don't want to seem pathetic, so I told her that you and I were thinking of getting married too."

Sage took a deep breath, feeling the warm water soothe her tense muscles. "Are you still in love with her or something?"

There was a long pause on the other end of the line.

"I don't know," Brian finally said.

"Be honest," Sage said. "If you are honest, I might just go along with it."

"You will?" Brian asked.

"Yup," Sage said. "I'll help you save face, but you must give me something in return."

"What?" Brian asked eagerly.

"We agree to break up, with no animosity involved," Sage said. "And you have to promise to be cordial about my next relationship."

"Wait a minute," Brian said. "I am still processing."

Sage let the silence stretch, giving Brian time to think. She rinsed the shampoo from her hair, her mind racing. This was her chance to set some boundaries and move forward.

"Are you serious?" Brian finally asked. "Would you really help me out with Natalia if we broke up amicably?"

"Yes," Sage replied firmly. "I think it's best for both of us. We've been drifting apart for a while, and it's time to be honest about that. You started dating me on the rebound."

"No," Brian protested.

"What did I say about being honest?" Sage asked sternly.

"Well, that may have been a part of it," Brian said sullenly, "but you are gorgeous. I wouldn't be a normal heterosexual male if I didn't find you attractive. I still do. And I don't just see you as a trophy girlfriend, either. I really do have fun with you. It's just that…"

"It has always been Natalia," Sage finished for him. "No one can replace her, no matter how you try."

"Well," Brian sighed heavily. "I guess you're right."

"Now, doesn't that make you feel better?" Sage chuckled. "When you admit it out loud."

"No, it doesn't make me feel better," Brian said. "Natalia is still going to marry that clown Shane. That's all she talks about every day."

"You and I don't talk every day, but yet you speak to her every day," Sage pointed out. "Even when we were in college, you spoke to Natalia every single night. I found it odd then, but you insisted that she was the one who called, and you were just friends, and you no longer had feelings for her blah blah blah. You remember that?"

"Vaguely," Brian inhaled.

Sage chuckled. "Well, I've got news for you, Brian. You have feelings for her. I'd even venture to say that her impending marriage is cutting you up inside. If you want me to help you save face, you must agree to us breaking up. It's long overdue."

"Okay, I agree," Brian said. "We'll break up, no hard feelings, and I'll be cool about your next relationship."

"Good," Sage said, relief washing over her. "And I'll tell Natalia what you want. But only this once, Brian. You should just come out and tell her how you feel and let the chips fall where they may."

Sage squeezed her eyes shut, thinking about giving advice she wouldn't even follow for herself. What would it be like to look Bruce in the eye and say, "I love you. I am attracted to you. It keeps me up at night. I want to be with you."

"Thanks, Sage," Brian intruded on her inner dialogue, his tone a mix of gratitude and resignation. "I appreciate you doing this for me."

"Wait, before you go," Sage said. "What would you think if I dated a guy way older than me? I mean, he could be old enough to be my father."

Brian chuckled. "So that's why you insist on me not saying anything about your next relationship."

"Yes," Sage hissed.

"I would wish you all the best," Brian said. "I gave you my word that I would be cool, didn't I?"

"You did," Sage said.

"Well, I am cool," Brian said.

Sage ended the call and finished her shower, feeling a surprising sense of freedom.

She dried off and dressed, then joined Bruce in the

kitchen, where he laid out dinner. Battery-operated candles illuminated the place, and the air was filled with the aroma of roasted chicken and garlic bread.

"Everything okay?" Bruce asked, noticing her happy expression.

"Yes," Sage said with a small smile. "I just handled something that's been hanging over me for a while. Brian and I have come to an understanding. We are over, finished, kaput. He even promised to be cool about my next relationship."

"Is that so?" Bruce looked at her curiously. "That's big of him. How did you manage that?"

"I told him I would go along with his attempts to make Natalia jealous."

"That's pretty childish," Bruce said.

"I was thinking the same thing," Sage said, "but I did secure my freedom and a confession that he had feelings for Natalia, and he said he would be cool with my next relationship."

Bruce shook his head. "I don't know if I should feel sorry for my son or applaud you for your negotiating skills."

"Applaud me, of course," Sage said. "I took your advice; I broke it off with Brian before I embarked on something else with someone else."

"Well then, let's eat and celebrate your newfound freedom." Bruce smiled. "And welcome to the single life club."

Sage smiled back. "Thanks, but I remember only too well not liking it much. When you are coupled up, you are less of a target for all the kooks out there. I think that's why I stayed with Brian for so long. Having someone around was far more convenient, even if the relationship wasn't perfect."

"You paint a grim picture of the dating world," Bruce said.

"Because it is grim," Sage said, "do you know how hard

it is to find a mature, intelligent guy in my age group who knows what he is about and not only thinking about sex? Someone I can be myself with, who isn't intimidated by my independence? Or act a fool when they discover that my mother is Anise Cooper? Or that my father is Paul Aubry?"

Bruce nodded. "I see your point."

"I accused Brian of using me to hide his feelings for Natalia, but I guess I used him, too, to hide from all the challenges of being single. The truth is, I was scared of being alone, of not finding someone who could handle me and my background. Whew, that was a mouthful," Sage said, taking her seat. Can we eat now? This looks amazing. Blossom is a beast in the kitchen."

Bruce smiled. "She is, I always think it's a waste that she didn't open a restaurant somewhere."

As they began to eat, the conversation flowed naturally. They talked about the farm, shared stories from their childhoods, and laughed over Bruce's humorous anecdotes.

Sage relaxed more with each minute, enjoying the simple pleasure of good food and company.

She sneaked glances at Bruce when she thought he wasn't looking. The man was handsome with his even white teeth, perfectly symmetrical face, and mesmerizing brown eyes. She wondered how long she could keep her feelings for him to herself.

"How many women have you dated?" she asked out loud.

Bruce stopped eating and looked at her, aghast. "You want a number?"

"I er... I am sorry," Sage said, horrified. "The thought came into my head and just slipped out of my mouth."

Bruce laughed. "That's usually how it works."

"But my filter," Sage moaned. "It slipped by my filter."

"Don't sweat it," Bruce said. "I promised you I'd tell you

whatever you want to know. I honestly can't remember the number of women I have dated. I can, however, remember the number of women I've had serious relationships with and why we broke up."

"Tell me," Sage said eagerly.

Bruce chuckled. "Alright, but you have to promise not to judge me too harshly."

Sage nodded, leaning forward in anticipation. "I promise."

"Well, there were three serious relationships," Bruce began. "The first was in college. Her name was Emily. We were young, and everything felt so intense and important. But as we grew, we realized we wanted different things. She wanted to travel and experience the world while I focused on building my business."

Sage listened intently, her heart pounding as she realized how much she wanted to know everything about him.

"The second was a few years after college. Her name was Laura. She was great, really driven and ambitious. But we were both so focused on our careers that we barely had time for each other. Eventually, we drifted apart."

"And the third?" Sage asked breathlessly.

Bruce sighed. "The third was Melissa. We were together for almost three years, and then she migrated. We mutually decided that we didn't want a long-distance situation, so we broke up."

"Thank you for sharing that with me." Sage cleared her throat. "I'll check my filter next time."

"Never. I have decided unilaterally to have filter-free conversations whenever we feel like it." He gave her a small smile. "Is that okay with you?"

"Fine," Sage nodded. "How old was Melissa?"

"A year older than I am," Bruce said. "Now, who is obsessed with age?"

"You've never dated a younger woman, have you?" Sage whispered.

"No," Bruce said. "I've always thought younger women were too immature. But then again, I went out with Lacy last weekend and she is my age, and I was not impressed by her maturity. So I guess it's the person and not the age. So, about you…" Bruce said, "how many serious relationships have you had?"

"Well, I had a serious boyfriend in high school. His name was Edward." Sage shrugged. "His father was a gangster, an area don. My sister Cinnamon got so concerned with my connection with the family she convinced my mom to send me to Mount Faith, out of Kingston and the radius of Edward. He was such a nice boy, too, and totally different from his father. He was a nerd, really. He wanted to be an astronaut. But we broke up after high school.

"And then I went Brian at Mount Faith, and you know how that went."

Bruce nodded. "I am familiar with that part of your life."

"Maybe the third time for me will be the charm," Sage said. "I am not interested in kissing too many frogs before I get my prince."

Chapter Fourteen

The electricity was still out when they finished eating.

"You have to admit there is an old-world romance to the flickering candles," Sage said while she cleared the table.

Bruce got up and helped.

"It is nice," he replied, stacking plates. "Reminds me of camping trips when I was a kid."

Sage smiled, the soft light casting shadows across her face. "I never went camping much. This is probably the closest I've been to roughing it."

Bruce laughed. "You missed out; you should camp outside at least once."

They worked in companionable silence for a few minutes; the only sounds were the clink of dishes and the soft crackle of the candles. When the table was clear, Bruce turned to Sage.

"So, what now?" he asked.

"Journal Two, by Dean Aubry," Sage said.

"Okay, I'll load the dishwasher and join you soon," Bruce said.

Sage took one of the candles and went to her room for the second journal. She held up the light to the book and opened the first page to make sure it was the right one.

Journal Entry # 30

My father insists that I marry Rosa Matthis. It is a good business move, he says. Her parents are the owners of a Union Bank in the town. It's a sensible match. The only problem is that Rosa is my friend Lionel's girlfriend, and I know for a fact that they are devoted to each other. But Lionel and Rosa are not from the same social class, that sort of thing is quite important to our set. A union between them would be frowned upon. He is illegitimate; as quiet as it's kept, he is my grandfather's son with the dressmaker in town. My father's unacknowledged brother. And he has no financial standing.

****

"Journal two is juicy," Sage said as she entered the living room. "I just read the beginnings of the first entry, and already I know there's going to be some mess."

Bruce chuckled, reclining on the settee and lying on cushions. "Well, if it is juicy, I won't fall asleep."

"I doubt you will," Sage said, sitting across from him and stretching her legs.

"Are your eyes okay for reading in the low light?" Bruce asked.

"This is quite bright," Sage replied, opening the journal and flipping back to entry thirty. She read what she had seen before.

Bruce snickered. "The Aubry family should have its own soap opera."

Sage nodded. "It's fascinating. Anyway, continuing."

Journal Entry #30 continued.

I find myself in a difficult position. My loyalty to Lionel, my childhood friend, is unwavering, but the pressure from my father is relentless. The stakes are high, and I can see the benefits this union with Rosa would bring to our family. Yet, the idea of betraying Lionel gnaws at me. How can I justify tearing them apart for the sake of business?

Every time I see Rosa and Lionel together, I see genuine happiness. Lionel's eyes light up in a way I've never seen before, and Rosa's laughter fills the room. They may not be a perfect match in society's eyes, but their bond is undeniable.

Last night, I overheard my father discussing the matter with Uncle Henry. They spoke of legacy, ensuring our family's future, and the importance of aligning with the Matthis family. Uncle Henry, always the pragmatist, agreed wholeheartedly. It felt as though they were planning my life without considering my feelings.

I tried broaching the subject with my mother this morning, hoping for support. But she, too, sees the advantages. "Sometimes we must sacrifice personal happiness for the greater good," she said.

My mind is a whirlwind of conflicting emotions. Do I follow my heart and stand by Lionel, or do I succumb to the pressure and marry Rosa? Either choice seems fraught with consequences.

****

"Wow," Bruce said when Sage finished reading.

"Obviously, I know he married Rosa, but what a dilemma."

"That's why they never smile in their pictures," Sage murmured. "I think my family is cursed on both sides."

Bruce chuckled. "Sage, people make decisions that seem right at the moment, but they often have to live with the consequences. It's not a curse, just a series of choices."

"I guess," Sage sighed. "But it feels like there's a pattern in our lives, a repeating cycle of duty over happiness, of practicality over love, of deviant sexual liaisons over normal, healthy relationships. Take my mother and father, for example. My mother was molested when she was barely in her teens by her own father. Then, my father married her because of her background, and he wanted access to my sister who was four at the time. In the process, my mother had us. And you know how that went. It has been one sick, twisted incident right after the other."

"Technically," Bruce pointed out, "from what I understand, correct me if I'm wrong, Anise's father was not Ronald Cooper. Greystone was her biological father."

"True," Sage nodded.

"So Greystone's main issue here was cheating on his wife and passing off the child of the affair onto another man."

"Yes," Sage said. "He loved my grandmother but stayed with his wife—duty over happiness."

"True," Bruce nodded.

"And they both had a successful wine business. He wouldn't upset the status quo, so practicality over love. Both grandfathers had the same patterns, ergo both sides of my family are plagued with making wrong choices.

"I even succumbed to it. I stuck with Brian for nearly two years because he was comfortable and undemanding, especially where sex was concerned. I feared change and thought staying with him would be easier than facing the unknown. But deep down, I knew I was settling.

"My relationship with Brian reflects my family's history of poor decisions and settling for comfort over true happiness. And the truth is if I never met…"

"You've gone silent," Bruce said after a long pause.

"I… er…" Sage cleared her throat. "I tend to rant, and I haven't finished reading."

"I don't mind your rants," Bruce said. "You do make a lot of sense. Reading these journals can lead to self-assessment, as you are finding out. Seeing the past through Dean Aubry's eyes can give you the insight to make different choices in your own life."

"I think writing down his life story and thoughts in an unfiltered manner is a brilliant idea," Bruce said. "His descendants will get to know him in a way that they wouldn't have otherwise. His experiences can guide you into not making the same blunders.

"In a way, that's what our elders were there for to guide us into not repeating their mistakes. But when you think about it, some older people are so ashamed of their choices and are caught up in saving face or appearing perfect that they hide their true stories. They present a sanitized version of their lives, which doesn't help us learn or grow."

"So true," Sage nodded. "I… that is so true."

"By being honest about our own mistakes and the lessons we've learned, we can break that cycle of shame and secrecy. Only through acknowledging our imperfections and sharing our real experiences can we truly help the next generation." Bruce said wistfully, "I wish I knew my grandparents' stories outside of the regular tame stories we often hear. I would love to know why my grandfather felt compelled to have a girl in every parish and why my grandmother put up with it.

"What made them tick, what were they thinking. When

I was young, they just seemed so old and tame. I could not picture them with full, interesting lives," Bruce said. "Maybe I should take a leaf out of Dean Aubry's book and write my own journal."

Sage chuckled. "Could I read it, please?"

"That would make me vulnerable to you," Bruce said. "You'd be privy to my inner thoughts."

"So I do my own journal, and we exchange," Sage suggested.

Bruce looked at her wordlessly for a long moment. "Do you know how intimate that would be, Sage?"

"I have an idea," Sage nodded.

"No, you don't," Bruce said. "There are people right now who have been partners or married for decades who have no idea what their spouse or partner is thinking or what they have thought, their dark fantasies or deep longings. I would have to wholeheartedly trust you, Sage Aubry, without reserve, to do something like that."

Sage took a deep breath, considering Bruce's words. "And I would have to trust you too. Maybe that's exactly why we should do it, to truly know each other beyond the surface."

Bruce's gaze softened. "It's a big step, Sage. Once we open that door, there's no going back. You just broke up with Brian today. Take a breath, live a little, enjoy your twenties. Trust me when I tell you these are the best days of your life."

"So you do know that you are the one I am in love with, don't you?" Sage breathed. "This is embarrassing."

"It doesn't have to be," Bruce closed his eyes. "Women have crushes on me all the time. What you think is love may very well be a crush. I am your boss, I don't look half bad, I practice good hygiene, and I am more mature than the boys you are used to."

Bruce cracked one eye open. "This will pass. We'll ignore it."

"And if it doesn't pass?" Sage raised an eyebrow.

"Then we write those journals and give them to each other to read," Bruce said. "Until then, can I hear more about Dean Aubry's interesting life?"

Sage took a deep breath, looked back at the journal, and asked, "I am curious. How did you find out about my feelings?"

"It's how you looked at me this morning," Bruce said. "I was jealous about the mystery guy you loved. I was striding to my office in a huff, and then I stopped and looked at you, and it clicked."

Sage inhaled raggedly. "I am officially mortified."

"Your feelings are not unreciprocated, Sage. I've been battling the same attraction to you for a while. In a perfect world, we'd be the same age and stage in life, and you wouldn't be my son's ex-girlfriend."

Sage's eyes widened. "But we aren't in a perfect world," she whispered.

"No, we aren't," Bruce agreed, his tone gentle but firm. "And that means we have to be realistic. This thing between us—it can't go anywhere. It's not fair to you, to Brian, or to me. At least not at this time. The timing would be off. That's not to say some time in the future. Maybe when you are a little older and more sure of your feelings."

"I am sure of my feelings," Sage scoffed. "They've been fixated on you for a year now. It was instant the moment I met you."

Bruce nodded. "I know, I felt it too."

"But sometimes feelings aren't enough," Bruce said softly. "Life is complicated, and relationships are even more so. We have to think about the consequences and the impact on the people around us."

Sage's eyes filled with tears, but she held his gaze. "So what now? Do we just pretend this never happened?"

Bruce took a deep breath, his expression pained but resolute. "We take a step back, give each other space. Focus on our respective paths and let time do its work. If it's meant to be, things will align when the time is right."

Sage wiped her eyes, nodding slowly. "And until then, we just... wait?"

"Until then, we live our lives," Bruce said. "Embrace the present, learn from our experiences, and grow. And who knows? Maybe someday, we'll be together."

Sage grinned. "Like the Supremes song?"

Bruce smiled. "Like the Supremes song. Now, tell me more about Dean Aubry. It might help take our minds off things."

Sage nodded, opening the journal again. "Where were we?"

"His loyalty to Lionel and his future marriage to Rosa," Bruce said.

"Oh yes," Sage started reading huskily. For now, Dean Aubry's life was a bit parallel to hers, and she wanted to see how he dealt with that.

Chapter Fifteen

Sage read entry after entry, Dean and Rosa's marriage, their hellish wedding night where Rosa confessed she was not a virgin and had been with Lionel before. Dean, contrarily, did not understand even though he had been playing with the girls in Bens Valley for years.

Journal Entry # 40

I am conflicted about my feelings for Rosa. Our marriage did not have the most auspicious beginning; we were not a love match. But the revelation on our wedding night that Rosa was not a virgin and had been with Lionel before me shattered my illusions of the woman I thought she was.

I am not proud of my reaction. I've spent years in Ben's Valley, flirting and playing with the girls, yet I never expected Rosa to have her own past. It's hypocritical, I know. I wanted her to be untouched, pure, something I could claim as mine alone. But she is not a possession. I am struggling to reconcile this double standard within myself.

Why am I feeling angry and confused? Ours is not a love match. Was I expecting too much? Is it fair to hold her to a different standard than I hold myself?

I wonder if our marriage can survive this turmoil. Can I move past my preconceived notions and fully and completely accept Rosa for who she is? Or will this revelation be the wedge that drives us apart? Only time will tell.

****

"Uh oh," Sage whistled. "What a hypocrite."

Bruce chuckled. "His attitude still rings true today, even for some men."

"What's your take on it?" Sage asked.

"I don't judge a woman by how many sexual partners she has had," Bruce said, "nor do I think she is some sort of prize if she hasn't had any. I believe it's the character and the choices people make that matter most. You can have a hellish relationship with a woman who has only been with you sexually and a satisfying and happy one with a woman who had sex with the whole village."

Sage laughed out loud. "How liberal of you, Mr. Whitlock, acknowledging the male and female double standards that exist in today's society. When it comes to sleeping around, men always get a pass, and if a woman dares to explore her sexuality, pass the smelling salts."

"Admittedly," Bruce said, "there are reasons why promiscuity in either sex is unattractive, but especially for women."

"Why?" Sage asked. "What's the reason why we gag when it's a woman who is promiscuous but give men a pass?"

"Well," Bruce said, "historically, women were seen as the gatekeepers of sex, responsible for ensuring the legitimacy of offspring. A woman's promiscuity was perceived as a threat to the social order because it created uncertainty around paternity. Men, on the other hand, were encouraged to spread their genes widely, which is why their promiscuity was more socially acceptable."

"But we aren't living in caves anymore," Sage countered. "Surely, we can evolve past that."

"True," Bruce nodded. "But societal norms and cultural beliefs change slowly. Even today, a woman's worth is often unfairly tied to her sexual behavior. In contrast, a man's worth is measured by different standards."

"Serious double standards," Sage muttered.

Bruce laughed. "It is a double standard even for me because I don't want to think of you with anyone, especially with Brian. Though I know I have no right to do so—you were his girlfriend for two years."

"Really?" Sage squeaked.

"Yep," Bruce said with a sigh. "What can I say? I understand Dean Aubry's hypocrisy."

Sage threw a pillow at Bruce. "I haven't had sex with anyone and most definitely not with Brian. My mother had no qualms about having the sex talk with us girls. She has always been frank about the whole thing. She just had one request of us: do not sell yourself short. Make sure you are ready to be vulnerable with another person before you embark on anything intimate. I haven't felt ready, so I don't push it, and Brian is the same. That's what I liked about him the most; he wasn't the type who wanted to rush into intimacy."

Bruce caught the pillow and held it, a thoughtful expression on his face. "I can't believe my parenting worked. I basically told him the same thing as your mother told you."

"Yup," Sage said, smiling. "My mother has been through a lot; her philosophy is that if she has made the mistakes already, there is no need for us to make them again. She has always emphasized that intimacy is about more than just the physical act. It's about trust, respect, and genuine connection. She wanted us to understand that and make choices that were right for us, not based on societal expectations or pressures."

Bruce nodded. "I think that's the best advice anyone could give a young person. It's about making choices that align with your values and what you truly want, not what others think you should do."

"Exactly," Sage agreed. "So, Mr. Whitlock, do you think I should continue reading, or should we have more of this sex talk?"

"Continue reading," Bruce chuckled. "Dean Aubry's life seems to have spurred some meaningful discussions. Maybe we'll have more."

Sage read way up into the night. They discussed all the interesting entries. When the light returned, she turned on the side lamp instead of the candle. Dean Aubry was discussing the birth of Horace.

Journal Entry #60

When Paul and Donna were born, I knew they were mine. When Horace came along, Rosa and I were not even pretending we were a couple. I was sleeping in the library suite, finding my sexual release in the arms of our downstairs maid. Rosa, I assumed, was living a chaste and sexless life.

Then she became pregnant, and I was stunned out of my complacency. "Whose child is it?" I asked accusingly.

"Lionel's, of course," Rosa said. "We started seeing each other when he visited from Britain last summer." She had no remorse in her tone. She was defiant. "You will treat this child like you would your others, which is not saying much. You barely give Paul and Donna any attention. In exchange, I will continue turning a blind eye to all the wickedness I know you do down here in the library with all the girls from the village and our young maid.

"You are a sick man, Dean Aubry, and if I had any sense at all, I would have left a long time ago. But my parents would only throw me out. They are so old-fashioned and fixed in their ways. They think I should stick with you and work things out when clearly we are over. I wish I had the mind to be an independent woman like my sister Justine!"

And so Horace was born. He, of course, looked like an Aubry. Lionel was an unacknowledged Aubry himself. Lionel came a year later for Horace's christening and stayed with us for the first time. He, Rosa, and their son lived upstairs for the summer, pretending that I didn't exist. And God forgive me, I didn't mind. I had a new dalliance, Krista Montova. I have never felt this way since Tessa Arlington. Suddenly, life was making sense again.

****

"Oh wow, Sage stopped reading. My goodness. This is the end of journal two."

Bruce chuckled. "How many journals are there?"

"Three," Sage yawned. "Do you think Horace will be shocked to find out he is not Dean Aubry's son?"

"Maybe not," Bruce said. "When we visited yesterday, he acknowledged that he was always different."

"Yep, probably knew it subconsciously," Sage said

sleepily. "I am tired. I will just close my eyes for a minute and then go to my room. I feel wiped out. This sofa is so comfy."

Chapter Sixteen

"**G**irl, your neck is going to hurt today with that position you're in," Blossom said, smiling and standing over her. "I see you stayed up reading."

"Yes," Sage sat up and yawned. "What time is it?"

"It's just after eight," Blossom said. "It doesn't look like it because it's still raining."

Sage rubbed her neck; it did feel a little tender. "Where is Bruce?"

"He has been up since the crack of dawn. He ate breakfast an hour ago and then left to visit a work site. He said to tell you that he'll be back by eleven to visit Horace Aubry."

"Yes," Sage nodded.

"Are you going to eat breakfast this morning?" Blossom asked.

"Yes, sure, I'll have fruits, nothing fancy." Sage nodded. "By the way, the dinner last night was good."

"Thank you," Blossom smiled and then pointed to the

journal. "Did you learn anything else about the murderous Dean Aubry? Did he kill anyone else?"

"Not so far," Sage said. "He and Rosa did not have a fairytale romance, though."

"Everyone knew that," Blossom shrugged. "They lived separate lives up at Aubry House. When he died twenty years ago, we joked that Miss Rosa finally killed him. But then again, there was your father and his court case."

"That was what finished him off, I think. It shamed him. His oldest son was in the news everywhere; people talked about it and compared them. So he took cover up at the house. Everybody was saying it was high time one of those Aubry men finally went to jail for molesting the underage girls in the valley."

"He spoke about flirting and playing with girls in the valley," Sage said. "It didn't occur to me that they were underage."

"Yes, they were," Blossom nodded. "It's probably genetics. Your father got it from his father who got it from his."

"I should check to see if pedophilia can be genetical," Sage murmured. "But in the case of the Aubrys, it is probably also learned behavior."

"Most definitely learned too," Blossom said. "Dean Aubry had a thirteen-year-old girl living up at Aubry House. He called her his adopted daughter. I remember her clearly now. He used to take her to church with him. She was such a cute little girl. She used to jump at her own shadow. She never spoke to the rest of us children at Sunday School. She called Mr. Dean Daddy, but she called Miss Rosa, Madam."

"She and Paul were the same age, but their relationship was odd. Even as a child, I could see that. She didn't associate with him like you would expect siblings to interact. She stuck to Dean Aubry like glue, holding his hand and acting shy. It was weird."

Blossom shook her head. "I had the niggling feeling that he was more to her than a father figure. I even overheard my parents talking about it. My dad said she had run away from her home, and Dean Aubry rescued her."

"Was her name Krista?" Sage whispered.

"Yes," Blossom nodded. "Krista. Did he mention her in his diary?"

"Yes," Sage said. "He said he was in love with her."

"Sick!" Blossom snorted. "Did he kill her too? One day, she just disappeared; she only stayed with them for a few months."

"He didn't say, I didn't read any more about Krista. I fell asleep."

"The things people got away with in the past," Blossom murmured.

"They still get away with it now," Sage said. "If my mother wasn't persistent, my father would never have gone to jail. There are still not many women like my mother in this country; people are more willing to turn a blind eye and hope someone else will do the reporting. Someone else will fix the issue. You just mind your own business and think that someone else will do something. I figure that's why the Aubry men got away with years of child sex abuse in Ben's Valley. There was no one willing to say something. Shame on all of you who stood by!"

"Dean Aubry mostly kept to himself when I lived in Ben's Valley," Blossom snorted. "I only heard stories."

"But what about my father, his son, Paul Aubry?" Sage asked. "He was around for years. You knew about him."

"I heard stories about him too," Blossom said stubbornly. "I can't go around accusing people of abuse when I didn't see it for myself.”

"Well, I hope if you actually see child sex abuse in your community now, you are willing to speak up and report it to the authorities no matter who the abuser is.”

"I am going to prepare your breakfast,” Blossom huffed and headed to the kitchen. "Are mangoes and pineapples okay? I have some dragon fruit, too.”

Sage looked at her suspiciously. "You know someone, don't you?”

"I do,” Blossom opened the fridge, her voice muffled.

"So why don't you report it?” Sage asked.

"Because it's none of my business,” Blossom said. "I've lived so long on God's earth because I mind my own business. He that keepeth his mouth keepeth his life. I am no informer.

"Besides, the people involved seem quite fine with their situation. She is fourteen with two children for a man of nearly thirty. Who am I to stick my mouth into a situation that has nothing to do with me? If I report them, who is going to feed her children?”

"Then men like my grandfather and father will always get away with their deeds,” Sage said sadly. "And if that is your attitude toward the current situation, you have absolutely no room to talk about the Aubrys one bit. Nobody in Ben's Valley who saw what the Aubry men did to their families, friends, and neighbors and kept their mouths shut has any reason to get on their soapbox and criticize them for how despicable they were.”

****

"You are quiet,” Bruce said to Sage as they drove out a few minutes after eleven. "Are you still thinking about your grandfather's diaries?"

"Not really," Sage said. "I am thinking about a lot of things. I had a conversation with Blossom this morning, and I am wondering if, by turning a blind eye to certain injustices, I am not just as bad as the perpetrator. And where does the needle move from social responsibility to plain old inquisitiveness?"

"Had I lived in Ben's Valley while my grandfather was alive, would I have done something? Or would I have excused it as 'Dean Aubry likes young girls' and let it pass? I am afraid of the answer."

Bruce glanced at Sage, his grip tightening slightly on the steering wheel. "That's a heavy question," he said. "But it's important to think about. Sometimes, we don't know how we would act until we're in the situation."

Sage nodded, her eyes fixed on the passing scenery. "After getting on my soapbox this morning with Blossom, accusing her of not doing anything to stop the abuse she sees going on in her community, I wonder if I would do things differently. I'd like to think I would err on the side of doing right, especially if I saw child abuse in my community, but would I really do something?"

Bruce nodded, his expression serious. "It's good that you're thinking about these things, Sage. It means you care about others. I couldn't see injustice and do nothing. I was a little social justice warrior back in high school because I just couldn't see bullying and pass it by.

"There was this boy, Tim Black. He acted feminine. He couldn't help it; that's just the way he was. But boy, was he a target. He was the butt of jokes and bullying, both at home and at school.

"I got my lip busted more than once for intervening for him. When my dad saw me come home the first time, he asked, 'Did you start the fight?' I said, 'No, it wasn't my fight; I was just defending Tim Black.' My dad looked at me proudly and said, 'You did the right thing, son. Standing up for others, especially when they can't stand up for themselves, is one of the most important things you can do. It takes courage, and I'm proud of you for having it.'

"That approval meant that whenever I saw injustice, even now, I never hesitated. I always did the right thing. And if the right thing is reporting it or intervening and getting a busted lip, then so be it."

"You know I can sense that in you," Sage smiled, her eyes softening. "And your dad sounds like a good man."

"He is," Bruce said, "He taught me that doing the right thing is often the hardest thing, but it's always worth it. So, to quote my father, Sage, do the right thing, let the world see, let the light shine everywhere, and when it seems like no one is watching, do the right thing anyway, do the right thing all the time."

Sage laughed, "That's the lyrics from Cobham and Bez's song Do The Right Thing. That was my high school graduation song. We had to practice it. I know it by heart."

"My dad said the whole song first," Bruce smiled.

Sage laughed out loud.

"That's what I like to see," Bruce said. "your laugh is refreshing."

****

Sage was in a much better mood when they drove up to Aubry House. Horace greeted them at the front door when they got there. Sage contemplated telling him he wasn't Dean Aubry's son but thought better of it. She would choose a different time. This was a business meeting, and she didn't want to throw him off.

She filmed both men as they discussed the plan. Horace was blown away by the attention to detail that Bruce gave the space. He was nodding like a marionette at every suggestion.

"I wouldn't change a thing," he said, pleased. "Not one thing. I knew it was a good choice choosing Whitlock Landscaping."

"That's a good sound bite," Sage joked. "Be sure to watch the first episode of Whitlock Landscapes to hear yourself say it."

Horace nodded. "I can't wait to see the finishing touches and to get myself featured, of course."

When they were leaving, Horace asked, "How are the journals going?"

"I, er," Sage stuttered.

"I'll wait in the car," Bruce said, walking ahead. "I have a phone call to make."

Sage turned to Horace. "I read two journals."

"And how bad was it?" Horace asked.

"Your father is Lionel Vicker," Sage said, "and there is a body buried under the mango tree. It's Tessa Arlington, and Dean Aubry was a pedophile like his son. He had a girl living here, Krista, who was just thirteen. She ran away from home, and he kept her as his lover."

"Oh, wow," Horace leaned on the balustrade on the veranda.

"Sorry to blurt it out so crassly," Sage said.

Horace shook his head like he was shaking something out of his ear. "I always knew Uncle Lionel was family, but just how close is blowing my mind. And as for Tessa Arlington, you mean that stuff was real?"

"Yes," Sage nodded. "He said it was an accident; his father told him to bury her under the mango tree."

"What happened to Krista?" Sage asked. "I am almost afraid to find out."

"Krista was officially adopted by my aunt Justine, my mother's sister. She was single and childless. I don't know what happened behind the scenes, but I heard that Justine came for her one day. Krista still keeps in touch. Whenever I go to Atlanta, I stay at her place. She is a retired teacher."

"Oh," Sage exhaled, "what a relief."

Horace sighed. "I am really going to have to read those diaries, aren't I?"

Sage nodded. "It gives you a lot of insight into the man that was your mother's husband."

"I am going to call Uncle Lionel," Horace said, "and let him know that I know."

"He is still alive?" Sage widened her eyes.

"Yes," Horace said. "He is eighty-six, lives on his own in the UK, and is quite healthy for his age. We speak every Sunday. He is hard of hearing, so I shout through the conversation. My God, I can't believe I am his son. This explains a few things, like why he insists on keeping in touch all these years. I can't even process it all now."

Sage nodded. "You going to be all right, Horace?"

"Yep," Horace nodded. "I'll have to be." He looked at his watch. "I have another meeting shortly. Keep on reading, Sage. If you find anything else of note, let me know."

Sage looked at him, worried. "Okay."

"I am fine," he smiled at her. "This sort of news is never easy, whatever your age, but I am far too busy now to dwell on it."

****

"You told him?" Bruce asked.

"Yes, I did," Sage said.

They watched as Horace got into his truck. He looked a little unsteady.

"Maybe I shouldn't have," Sage said.

"I would have wanted to know," Bruce said. "His parents, both biological and otherwise, should have said something. But the people in the Silent Generation were great secret keepers."

Sage chuckled softly. "And my generation overshares on the internet. Could it be that we have something right?"

Bruce chuckled. "Maybe a middle ground is best."

"So what's next?" Sage asked.

"We'll have to go to Garrick's office to print the plan and use the internet."

"Can we drive through Ben's Valley?"

"Sure," Bruce said. "I figure you've read about it so much you'd want to see it."

Sage nodded. "I'll maybe see some of my unacknowledged relatives at the side of the road. I'll take some pictures too to show my sister. She will be curious because I will have to tell her about all of this."

Bruce nodded.

He descended the hill and into Ben's Valley. On the outskirts of the town, there was evidence of small farms and colorful houses.

"Horace's new venture will give a well-needed boost to this area," Bruce said. "Quite a few people leave Ben's Valley to look for work in Ocho Rios."

Ben's Valley had a sleepy little town square with a handful of shops, a post office, and an Anglican church that looked like it hadn't changed in decades.

The town square was a hub of activity, with vendors

selling fruits, vegetables, and handmade crafts. The scent of jerk chicken wafted through the air from a nearby food stall, making Sage's mouth water.

They passed a group of teenagers gathered around a small radio, listening intently to a reggae tune and then challenging each other to a dance-off. Bruce waved at them, and they waved back enthusiastically.

There was a bronze statue of Benjamin Aubry, the man who gave the town its name. Bruce slowed down and allowed her to take pictures.

"This looks nothing like his pictures at the house," Sage giggled.

"You are right. Isn't that a smile on his face?" Bruce said. "This guy looks pleasant."

"That's the difference," Sage nodded.

Bruce pointed out various landmarks as they headed out of the town square. "That's Miss Enid's shop. They make the best patties in town. And over there is the Dean Aubry High School."

"They named a high school after Dean Aubry?" Sage frowned. "How come I didn't know of it?"

"That high school has been around for a while," Bruce said, "long before I was born."

She leaned out the window, trying to capture everything on video.

As they reached the edge of town, Bruce turned the car towards Garrick's office. Sage looked back at Ben's Valley, feeling a sense of nostalgia as if she was seeing the town through the eyes of a person who had been there before.

"Why am I even feeling like this?" Sage asked out loud. "A sense of déjà vu so powerful I feel as if I don't want to leave."

"Because of the journals, despite yourself, you are getting

immersed in Dean Aubry's life," Bruce said. You should read it in short spurts and not in huge chunks. His life story can be overwhelming."

"I am getting used to it," Sage said to Bruce. "Is it overwhelming for you?"

"I can handle it," Bruce said. "Round three tonight?"

"Yep," Sage nodded. "Surely things can't get any worse, can they?"

Chapter Seventeen

Garrick Whitlock's office was on top of a hill overlooking St. Ann's Bay. It seemed as if it had been a house converted into a workspace. The residential area had given way to commercial spaces on both sides of the road.

There was an unfettered view of the sea. When they arrived, Garrick was on his way out. He was a lighter-skinned, bigger version of Bruce.

"Nice to meet you, Sage," he said briskly after they were introduced. "Wish I could stay to chat, but I have a meeting with a client, and I am running a bit late. The back office is available. If you need anything, ask Natalia."

"Natalia works here?" Sage asked Bruce when they went inside. "The Natalia? Brian's ex?"

"Yes," Bruce nodded. "Did I fail to mention that? She is the office manager."

There was a long corridor leading from the reception area. To the right were private offices, and to the left were cubicles. Bruce seemed to know his way around. They passed one of the glass offices, and the lady inside waved. She was on the phone.

"That's Natalia," Bruce said.

Sage slowed down a bit and stared. Natalia stared back. She was cute—an older version of the picture in Bruce's room, minus the pigtails. She had her hair in a pixie cut and sported a nose ring. From what Sage could see from her top upwards, she was big-busted.

Sage dragged her eyes from Natalia and caught up with Bruce, who had entered the office at the very end. It had a desk, a chair, and two guest chairs before the desk. The blinds were open exposing a gorgeous view.

"This is quite the view," Sage said. "How am I going to get anything done?"

"You'll get used to it," Natalia said behind her.

Sage spun around. "Oh, hey."

Natalia was a lot shorter than she had expected and top-heavy. She was dressed in black pants and a pinstripe top.

"Hello," Natalia said. "You look better than your picture."

"Thank you," Sage said.

"When I saw you first, I thought Brian had taken a stock photo of some supermodel to make me jealous."

Bruce cleared his throat. "Why am I being ignored here? Am I the invisible man?"

Natalia grinned. "Uncle Bruce," she went over and hugged Bruce. "I apologize. It's my first time meeting Sage. Forgive me for ignoring you."

Bruce grinned. "You are forgiven."

"I am going off to lunch. Would any of you like to join me?"

Sage was hungry. She had only had fruits earlier at the house.

"Where exactly are you going for lunch?" she asked.

"Downstairs, we have a kitchen and our own cook," Natalia said.

"I am going to get cracking on this," Bruce pointed to his computer. "Bring me back something."

"Sure," Natalia answered first.

****

"I can't believe I am eating with my ex-boyfriend's girlfriend," Natalia said. "The gorgeous Sage. Brian is always going on and on about you."

"Oh really," Sage said. "I could say the same thing about you."

"He talks about me to you?" Natalia widened her eyes.

"Yes," Sage nodded.

"Congratulations on the marriage, by the way," Natalia said. "Brian told me you two were going to tie the knot as soon as he gets back from college, and he wasn't going to wait."

Sage nodded, feeling deceitful. "I guess the same congratulations are in order for you and what's his name?"

"Shane." Natalia looked at her sheepishly. "I am not getting married to Shane."

"You aren't?" Sage raised her eyebrows. "But your impending marriage has been driving Brian crazy."

"Really?" Natalia laughed. "I didn't know that it worked. I made up the whole thing to get him back. I see it backfired. Now he is getting married to you."

"No, he is not," Sage chuckled. "He made up the marriage to save face with you."

"And you went along with it?" Natalia asked. "Why?"

"Because he and I are no longer together. We broke up.

But he is still my friend."

"Get out of here," Natalia leaned forward. "Are you serious?"

Sage nodded. "Serious."

Natalia smiled. "I like you."

"I was thinking the same about you," Sage said. "So when are you and Brian going to stop playing games with each other?"

"I am going to make him suffer a bit," Natalia said.

Sage laughed. "But I thought you were the one who made him suffer with your relationship with Shane."

"I never had a relationship with Shane," Natalia said. "I only told Brian that when he showed me your picture. I was jealous. I didn't even have much time to make up a love interest, so I used Shane, who was quite fine to go along with it once I bought him a patty and a drink when I was at his shop detailing my car."

Sage chuckled.

"And then it mushroomed from there. I never wanted to break up with Brian, but we had this stupid quarrel, and then next thing I know, we were declaring things over, and he met you."

"The rebound girl," Sage said. "Yay, me."

"Well, you don't look like a rebound girl," Natalia said. "When I saw your picture first, I went home and cried."

Sage smiled. "Really?"

Natalia nodded. "Yeah, really. I was convinced he had moved on to someone amazing."

"Funny, I think that's exactly what Brian wanted you to think," Sage chuckled. "But he always talked about you when we were together. My goodness, sometimes it got annoying."

Natalia smiled wider and wider. "Do you think it's too late

to fix things with him?"

"No," Sage said. "what's your plan?"

Natalia looked thoughtful. "I'll start by being honest with him. No more games, just the truth. When he comes back out here, though, I don't want to do it over the phone."

Sage nodded. "Sounds like a good start. Honesty might actually get you what you both really want."

Natalia smiled. "Thanks, Sage. I am so happy I met you and look how apprehensive and jealous I was about meeting you."

"When there was no need to be," Sage shrugged. "I hope it works out for you two."

"Thanks." Natalia nodded.

Chapter Eighteen

It was a whirlwind two weeks. She and Bruce had worked out a schedule. She would film the preparation stage of his landscaping project during the day and edit the raw footage at Garrick's office in the evening.

After they had eaten dinner together, they spent time reading Dean Aubry's journal and discussing the finer points of his entries. When work started in earnest at Aubry House, they got even busier. Sage went to Kingston for Cayenne's dress fitting and faithfully reported all she had learned about their family background. They were both lying on opposite settees in the half-dark, catching each other up on their week.

"Oh, my goodness," Cayenne breathed when Sage was finished talking. "Our family is rotten to the core."

"Horace is okay," Sage said.

"Maybe I should clarify," Cayenne chuckled. "Our family, meaning Dean Aubry's direct descendants, are rotten to the core."

"Speak for yourself," Sage murmured. "I am not rotten. I am Sage. I was born to purify the lineage."

Cayenne laughed.

"And we can't choose which family we were born into, but we sure can choose what sort of family we will create," Sage said. "I know your life with Lance will be a good one. You'll create a different sort of history. Your grandchildren will have nice things to say about you two."

"Thank you," Cayenne said. "I am raising an imaginary glass to that toast."

"Clinking my imaginary glass to yours," Sage said.

"So, how is it going with you and Bruce?" Cayenne asked. "With all that proximity, I expected that your crush would have crashed by now and that you'd find out he is not as desirable as you had thought."

"On the contrary," Sage said, "he is all that and more. And for your information, I didn't just have a crush on him. I was in love with him."

"So you are not in love with him anymore?" Cayenne turned to face her.

"Of course I am," Sage said. "And he knows; he figured it out. And he said we should take our time about it. He dates with purpose, and I don't think he is too sure about dating me. I am too young for him, I guess. He said he'd date a younger woman, but she'd have to be special."

"But you are special," Cayenne said. "How dare Bruce Whitlock!"

Sage giggled and then sobered up. "You can't force a man to love you, Cayenne. He has to think I am extraordinary to take the risk. I understand that. It's such a pity that I already blabbed that I am in love with him.

"I don't want his pity or a charity relationship. I want him to genuinely want to be with me. I wouldn't be interested in anything else.

"So, if he wants marriage and a family?" Cayenne asked. "What would you do?"

"Jump at the chance," Sage said. "I just want to be with him and no one else. I am that sure about my feelings. He is convinced I can't be because I am in my twenties. Plenty of women get married in their twenties, don't they? And stay together with their partner, right?"

"Right," Cayenne nodded. "Of course. I am getting married in my twenties. And I know loads of people who are still together after many years. If you are compatible from the get-go, the only other place to go is up. You grow deeper in love, spend time together, build a life together, and support each other through everything. It's about the connection and commitment. The two Cs of marriage, according to the marriage counselor, Lance and I are seeing."

"Exactly," Sage agreed. "And I feel that connection with Bruce. It's frustrating that he can't see it the same way yet."

"Give him time," Cayenne said. "Sometimes people need a little longer to come around, especially if they've been hurt before or are cautious about such a big step. And when they come around, they go all in."

"I hope you're right," Sage sighed. "I'm willing to wait, but it's hard not knowing if he'll ever feel the same way."

"I'll check him out for you," Cayenne said. "Take him as your plus one to the rehearsal dinner in two weeks."

"When you say check him out, you mean you will quiz him about his feelings for me?" Sage asked suspiciously. "Because that would be too embarrassing."

"No," Cayenne said. "I would never. Mom, Nana, and Grandma Saidie will be there for that."

"Ooh," Sage said, "Grandma Saidie can get a read on him.

Mom said, if I want a good read on a man, take him to see Grandma Saidie."

"Yup, she told me that, and that's why I took Lance to see her," Cayenne said. "I got her full approval. She loves him."

"Good," Sage nodded. "I hope Bruce says he'll come as my plus one. I'll ask him when he comes to pick me up tomorrow."

"Too bad you'll be getting your new car in a couple of days," Cayenne chuckled. "No more long drives with him to St. Ann."

****

Bruce was sitting in the Landry's pool lounger. Jackie had invited him to a barbecue after Jackie found out he was spending the weekend in Kingston.

"Don't say no," Jackie had warned. "I told all the project managers not to bother you for the evening. You need to relax with your friends sometimes. Besides, Carl said he is longing to have a chat with you. Come early before the crowd."

So here he was, bullied into relaxing by his office manager.

There weren't many people there at this hour. In fact, they were just setting up. Twelve-year-old Madison was the deejay and was testing out her songs. Jackie flitted in and out of the house with food containers while the other children were splashing around in the pool.

"Maddie!" Jackie yelled. "Use the playlist marked appropriate for children."

"But it's only old songs!" Maddie yelled back.

"Play them," Jackie growled, then waved at Bruce. "Just another day here in Landry land."

Bruce grinned.

Carl plopped down beside him and handed him a soft drink. "So, how's it going in St. Ann?"

"Good," Bruce murmured, pushing his shades on his forehead.

"Jackie has me watching your weekly videos," Carl said. "I can't believe I find them interesting. I anticipate seeing what the men are going to do next."

Bruce laughed.

"I didn't realize Brian's girlfriend was so pretty," Carl said. "She made that cameo in the second video. I was like, hold up, that's the girl? How on earth did Brian pull her?"

"They broke up," Bruce said. "And I have been seriously considering dating her myself."

Carl whistled. "Just considering? I'd be all over her like white on rice if I were you, lonely and single."

Bruce groaned. "I am alone but not lonely."

"So I take it you would have no qualms about the age difference, the fact she was dating your son, any of it."

"Nope, no qualms." Carl sipped his drink. "Have you told Brian you will be dating his ex?"

"No," Bruce sighed. "It's a conversation I am not looking forward to having with him."

"Then don't have it," Carl said, "not unless you are serious about her and she is going to be his potential stepmother or something."

"I was thinking along those lines," Bruce said. "I have feelings for Sage. I have been trying to suppress them and act like they are not there, but I haven't been successful."

"I tried the same thing with Jackie after we met," Carl nodded. "You remember we went to that civic society function? I didn't even talk to her. Just one look, and I started getting itchy around my heart."

Bruce chuckled. "I remember, but you were with Denise

at the time."

Carl sighed. "Yup, and I waited for my feelings for Jackie to pass. They never did. Six months later, we were married. Thirteen years later, I would do it again. Suppressing feelings never usually works."

"Even if there are valid reasons for doing it?" Bruce asked.

"Valid reasons like?" Carl raised an eyebrow.

"The age gap," Bruce said.

"She is how old?" Carl asked.

"Twenty-two," Bruce said.

"I married Jackie when she was twenty-two," Carl said.

"But you were five years older," Bruce said. "Don't be obtuse. I don't want to be the old man with the young gorgeous wife who leaves me for someone more her age when she finally wakes up and sees me for the old man that I am."

"If she returns your feelings, that won't happen," Carl said. "She'll be just as committed as you are. People who marry for money or status usually leave their partner in an age-gap situation. Sage Aubry is both a Greystone and an Aubry. She does not need money or status."

Bruce sighed.

"You are going to overthink this and let her move on," Carl said. "What are you going to do? Wait until she is thirty before you date her? The age gap will still be there. It will never shrink."

"You make valid points," Bruce said.

"But you are still not going to pounce. I know you," Carl sighed. "I think Sage would be good for you."

"You haven't even met her," Bruce said.

"But Jackie has," Carl said, "and she thinks she is perfect for you."

"So that's what this invitation is about," Bruce laughed.

"Jackie wanted you to talk me into dating Sage. To what end, I gather?"

"Well," Carl grinned sheepishly. "Natalia and Jackie were talking. Natalia says Sage looks at you with adoration when she thinks no one is looking. She watches how you interact in Garrick's office and thinks there is something there."

"I see where this is going," Bruce murmured. "Natalia is making sure there are no obstacles in her way when Brian gets back. Smart girl."

"That's what I said," Carl chuckled. "So, are you going to give it a shot?"

Bruce leaned back in his chair, staring at the sky. "I don't know, Carl. I mean, she's great. She's smart and funny, and we get along well. But the age difference... it's a lot."

Carl shrugged. "Age is just a number, man. If you both feel something, why not explore it? Besides, you could use a little happiness in your life."

Bruce sighed, putting his shades back over his eyes. "I'll think about it."

"That's all I'm asking," Carl said. "Just give it a chance. You might be surprised."

Bruce smiled weakly. "We'll see. For now, let's just enjoy the evening."

Carl nodded, raising his bottle. "To possibilities."

Bruce clinked his glass against Carl's, feeling a glimmer of hope amidst his doubts. Maybe Carl was right. It may be worth taking a chance with Sage.

Chapter Nineteen

Bruce came to pick her up the next morning. It was a little after six. It was shaping up to be a bright day, and it was already humid.

"I have good news," Sage turned to him. "My car is here in Jamaica, but it's not cleared from customs yet. The dealer said next week. So you won't have to pick me up next weekend."

"I am happy for you," Bruce said, "and kind of saddened. I liked hanging out with you on our drives. It's pathetic how I missed you this weekend."

"You did?" Sage smiled widely. "I thought you were keeping me at arm's length."

"I am done with arm's length," Bruce said. I am ready to rub shoulders."

Sage laughed. "And what does that entail?"

"An upgrade from snail's pace," Bruce said, looking at her intently.

"To what, then?" Sage asked, her voice softening.

Bruce moved closer; his eyes locked on hers. "To this," he whispered, gently cupping her face. He leaned in slowly, giving her time to pull away if she wanted to. But she didn't. She closed her eyes as their lips met in a tender, lingering kiss. The world around them seemed to fade away, leaving just the two of them in that moment.

When they finally pulled back, both were breathing a little heavier, hearts pounding. Sage's eyes fluttered open, and she saw the same mixed emotions she felt reflected in Bruce's gaze.

"That," he said softly, "is what rubbing shoulders entails."

Sage smiled, her cheeks flushing. "I think I like this upgrade."

"So, how was your weekend?" he asked.

"I hung out with my sisters, mainly Cayenne," she said, her voice breathless. "She… er… said I should invite you to her reception dinner."

"So that your family can vet me?" Bruce chuckled.

"Well, yes. How did you guess?" Sage asked.

"It's the way of things," Bruce said. "I'd love to come."

"Great," Sage said, turning to look at him. "It's a whole weekend thing. You could be my plus one at the wedding too."

"Okay," Bruce nodded.

Sage exhaled. "I didn't expect you to say yes."

"Because you are unsure of my feelings for you," Bruce said, "or how deep I want to take this?"

"Yes!" Sage said.

"We'll take our time," Bruce said. "There is no rush."

****

In the ensuing weeks, Sage could only think about the kiss. The project consumed most of her and Bruce's time and that intimacy was never repeated. It was as if Bruce was putting some distance between them.

They had maintained their evening ritual of walking together on the farm, whether it rained or not. She had met his entire family by now. They didn't find it odd that Brian's ex girlfriend seemed so close to Bruce.

"Your father didn't bat an eyelid when he saw us holding hands," Sage said as they walked past the workers' cabins.

"He wouldn't say anything to you," Bruce said. "He thinks you are pretty, and he did wonder how Brian would take your switch of affections."

"He said he would be cool with it," Sage said.

Bruce grimaced. "He won't be. I am anticipating a meltdown when he gets here next week."

"I didn't remember he was coming back next week," Sage said, then stopped.

The thought occurred to her that if Brian had a meltdown, as Bruce had said and asked him to choose, she would be toast. "You'd choose him over me, wouldn't you?" she asked, her eyes wide. "I mean, it makes sense. He's your son. I'm just a girl who would come between you two. Bros before hos, blood is thicker than water, family ties are the strongest, and family is forever…"

She was searching for more words, but Bruce gently placed a finger on her lips, stopping her.

"Sage, stop," he said softly. "It's not that simple. Yes, Brian is my son, and I love him. But that doesn't mean your feelings and our connection doesn't matter. We'll handle whatever comes our way together."

Sage looked into his eyes, searching for reassurance. "But what if he can't handle it? What if he makes you choose?"

Bruce took her hands in his, squeezing them gently. "Then we'll cross that bridge when we come to it. But know this: I care about you, Sage. Deeply. We'll find a way."

He pulled her closer to him. "I like hanging out with you. You are a breath of fresh air in my life."

Sage felt her heart race as she looked into his eyes, seeing the sincerity and warmth there. "I feel the same way, Bruce."

Without another word, Bruce leaned in, closing the distance between them. His lips found hers in a tender yet passionate kiss, conveying their emotions and unspoken promises. Sage melted into the kiss, wrapping her arms around his neck, feeling the world around them fade away.

When they finally broke apart, both were breathless, their foreheads resting against each other.

Bruce smiled, brushing a strand of hair from her face. "Together," he whispered.

Sage nodded, her eyes shining. "Together," she echoed.

They continued their walk hand in hand.

Chapter Twenty

"**D**o you want to hear the last entry in Dean's diary?" Sage asked as they cuddled together on the settee. "Or watch a movie?"

"I don't know," Bruce said, rubbing his hand along her arm. "I'm not in the mood to be depressed. His later entries are so dark."

"He was unhappy," Sage said, reaching for the journal. "He didn't live much of a fulfilled life. His children don't talk to him unless they have to. He has to practically dangle money before them to make them come to Sunday dinner. His wife is grieving her lover, Lionel, who got married and moved on with his life. The people in Ben's Valley are giving him a wide berth since the public court case against his son Paul. Oh, and no maid under fifty will work at Aubry House, and they keep their children away."

"Poor thing," Bruce said sarcastically. "His life of debauchery is falling apart."

"You reap what you sow," Sage murmured. "He could have been a better person than his father. Anyway, here it is, entry number one hundred."

Journal Entry #100

I am dying. My prognosis is not good. Man was allotted three score and ten years and by reason of strength, perhaps more. Yet here I am, facing the end much sooner than I had ever anticipated. The weight of this reality presses heavily on my heart, and the days seem to blend into one another as I grapple with the knowledge of my impending departure.

As I reflect on my life, I am filled with mixed emotions. There are moments of joy and laughter that I hold dear, memories of loved ones, and experiences that shaped me. But there are also regrets, mostly regrets, paths not taken, and words left unsaid. It's strange how clarity comes with such intensity in the face of death. The trivial worries and petty grievances that once occupied my mind now seem insignificant.

The women I've loved, the ones I've defiled, and the ones I've used continue to haunt me every day. I want to say sorry to each one of them. I will leave a cash donation to each of them in my will. I know that won't compensate for the devastation I left in their lives, but at least it's something.

To the Arlington family, Tessa's body is under the mango tree. I never killed her; it was all an accident. The horror of that night will be etched in my memory forever. I should have said something to the family. It is wrong to have kept silent in your grief. I know you will not forgive me for my silence, but the guilt of that night has shadowed my soul ever since. And I have never had a happy day since.

I have wronged my son, Paul, my firstborn, so badly.

My actions have cast a long, dark shadow over his life. I was never the father he deserved. Instead of guidance and love, I offered criticism and neglect. My choices and failures have left him scarred, struggling to find his way, emulating my attitude toward women. He was sentenced to prison for hurting his own daughters; I think that should have been my sentence, too. His crime is my crime. Not only have I covered for Paul all these years, but I did the same things he did. May God have mercy on us both.

To Donna, my dear daughter, I am sorry we were never close and that you always searched for approval in all the wrong places, leading you to choose a partner who mirrored my flaws. I see now how deeply my failings as a father have impacted you. You deserved a father who would support and uplift you, not one whose absence and indifference left you feeling unloved and unworthy.

I regret not being there to guide you, help you understand your worth, and show you what a healthy relationship looks like. Instead, you found someone who, like me, failed to recognize and cherish the incredible person you are. I am profoundly sorry for the pain and confusion my actions have caused you.

To Horace, though you were not my son, you were still my relative, and I was duty-bound to provide for you. Yet, in many ways, I failed you too. Perhaps it is good that you were not mine by blood, for my failings might have weighed even heavier on your heart, and my proclivities might have been a burden on you like they were Paul's. Nonetheless, I should have been a better guardian, a better mentor. I ignored you for most of your life. Fortunately, that might have made you a better person, and I am pleased with the man you've become.

To Rosa, through the years, I have developed a certain fondness for you that can only come from living together and weathering life's storms. Though our union was fraught with infidelity on both sides, more mine than yours, and constant battles that wore us down, there were also moments of tenderness and understanding that I will always cherish.

Despite the betrayals and the pain we inflicted on each other, you remained steadfast in my life. Your resilience and strength, even in the face of my many failures, have always astounded me. I regret not valuing you more and not being the husband you deserved. My actions have caused you so much hurt; I am deeply sorry.

In the quiet moments, when the chaos of our conflicts subsided, I saw the depth of your love and commitment. You stood by me, even when I gave you every reason not to. Your unwavering dedication is something I have come to appreciate more than words can express.

As I reflect on our years together, I regret how I treated you and the opportunities for happiness that I squandered. I wish I had been a better partner who supported and uplifted you instead of dragging you down.

Rosa, you are a remarkable woman, and I am grateful for the time we shared, even if it was far from perfect. I hope you can forgive me for the pain I caused and find peace in your heart. You deserve all the happiness and love that I failed to give you.

To my grandchildren, I urge you to break the cycle of dysfunction in our family. My advice to you is to prioritize open communication and genuine understanding. Don't be afraid to express your feelings and listen actively to each other. Respect and empathy are the cornerstones of healthy relationships.

Seek to understand before seeking to be understood. Avoid making assumptions and always give each other the benefit of the doubt. When conflicts arise, approach them with the willingness to resolve and heal rather than blame or win. Remember that forgiveness is a powerful tool, not just for others but also for yourself.

Cultivate a sense of unity and support within the family. Celebrate each other's successes and offer a helping hand during tough times. Encourage each other to pursue dreams and aspirations and be there to uplift one another when the going gets tough.

Lastly, always remember the importance of self-care and self-love. A healthy relationship with yourself sets the foundation for healthy relationships with others. Take time to reflect, grow, and invest in your personal well-being.

Break the cycle, my dear grandchildren, and create a legacy of love, respect, and harmony. You have the power to shape our family's future, and I believe in each one of you.

Lastly, I seek forgiveness from all those I have wronged and offer my deepest gratitude to all those I have loved. My time is nearly done, but I hope that I can find some measure of redemption in these final moments. May God have mercy on my soul.

****

"Now that is excellent advice," Bruce said huskily, "from a man who has led a life that was less than exemplary."

Sage's eyes were filled with tears, but she blinked them away. "I… er… I need a moment to process."

Bruce nodded. "I understand."

"I will type this up and email it to all the Aubrys. I'm going to ask Horace for their email addresses. The family needs to read this."

"Good for you, Sage," Bruce murmured. "Dean Aubry may have created a way for his family to be whole because of his honesty. And that being said, I'll have to discuss with Horace how to proceed with cutting the mango tree."

"I think the Arlington family and the authorities should be notified, too, if we are going to find bones under there," Sage said.

"Yes," Sage nodded. "I'll definitely have to include parts of this in the documentary now."

Chapter Twenty-One

They were calling it the mango tree episode. Horace had permitted her to air parts of the last journal entry on Bruce's landscape channel. It had gone viral. The local media were interested in the Aubry story: the death of Tessa, her grave under the mango tree.

A feature on Ben's Valley, its residents, and the Aubrys of Aubry House had aired in a prime-time news slot on local television. Once again, the Aubrys were the family name on everybody's lips.

Bruce had scheduled an early morning removal of the mango tree to reduce the number of onlookers that their sudden fame would certainly draw. But even then, the place was filled with onlookers when they drove up. The police had cordoned off the area, a coroner was on standby, and there was an air of anticipation at the tree's removal.

"I have gotten more exposure from this job than from all my other jobs combined," Bruce looked across at her as she fiddled with her equipment. "I have more job offers than I have staff. I am going to have to expand. And it's all because of you."

Sage chuckled. "That's right. At this point, I should be asking for shares in your company, a promotion, and a corner office beside yours. I wouldn't mind my own projects either. I think I have a pretty good handle on what you do after creating this docuseries."

Bruce turned to her. "Okay, I'll start you off on something small and see how you handle it. Maybe a quarter acre."

Sage looked at him wide-eyed. "I was only half joking."

"You made some excellent suggestions for this garden," Bruce said. "You have a good eye for design. I'll see what I can do about shares in the company and an office beside mine. I think over time, all of that will be a given anyway."

"What do you mean?" Sage whispered.

Bruce smiled and cupped her cheek. "Lady, you have crept under my skin and into my heart. I don't want to imagine a day without you in it. I don't even care about our age difference anymore. I think we make a pretty good team, professionally and personally."

Sage felt her heart race. She reached up and covered his hand with hers, looking into his eyes.

"Bruce, I... I don't know what to say."

"Then don't say anything," Bruce replied softly, leaning closer. "Just know that whatever happens, from here on out, I'm here for you. We'll take this one day at a time."

Before Sage could respond a chainsaw roared to life. The tree removal crew was ready to begin. Bruce gave her a reassuring squeeze on the shoulder. "It's showtime."

Sage scrambled out of the car. She needed a good spot to set up her equipment and capture the momentous event. Tessa Arlington's remains were found, as expected, under the mango tree.

It was all over the midday news when Bruce dropped her home that afternoon. She needed time to edit the footage she had gathered so far and to incorporate it into the weekly footage.

Blossom was watching the television with rapt attention when Sage sat down at the nook.

"Tough day?" Blossom turned down the television and looked at her.

"Yes," Sage nodded. "But revealing too."

She smiled softly as she remembered what Bruce had said to her. She hadn't stopped replaying it in her head.

"My family is grateful to you for reading the journals," Blossom said. "If you hadn't, who knows when we would have discovered what really happened to Tessa."

"You are most welcome," Sage nodded.

"What would you like for lunch?" Blossom asked. "Anything your heart desires, I will whip it up for you."

"Some of your roast beef sandwiches would be nice," Sage licked her lips.

"Done," Blossom nodded.

"How much longer will this project take?" Blossom asked as she served lunch and sat across from her. "I've been watching the series on my phone. I am anxiously awaiting the reveal."

Sage laughed. "One more month. Horace is done with the house renovations, so Bruce will tackle the gardens in that area shortly. The guys are just putting in the infinity pool on the back patio, and the gazebo is just about ready. Bruce is overseeing the installation of some mature trees today, and the arborists are coming to check on the health of the existing plants. By the end of the month, the outdoor space will be a paradise."

Blossom nodded. "That's wonderful news. I can't wait to see it all come together. The reveal is going to be spectacular."

"Indeed it will," Sage agreed. "Everyone's hard work is paying off. It's going to be a sight to behold. Horace said he is already getting queries for bookings."

Blossom nodded. "How is he taking the news that he wasn't Dean Aubry's son?"

"Good," Sage said, biting into her sandwich. "I told him a few weeks ago, so he was prepared. He has always known that he is different. Nothing much has changed with this revelation."

Blossom nodded. "The other day you made me think when you asked me about turning a blind eye to child abuse in my community."

Sage nodded. "I remember."

"I called child protection services on the couple I told you about," Blossom sighed. "I made an anonymous report."

"That's awesome," Sage grinned.

"I don't know what will come of it, but it was the right thing to do," Blossom said. "My conscience bothered me so much after that conversation with you that I had to do something. I realized that I was one of those people who would find fault with the most inconsequential things, like the length of skirts, but I had no trouble ignoring illegal things in my community, like electricity stealing and men sleeping with underage girls. I used to ignore issues like illegal dumping and domestic violence."

"That doesn't mean I will report every little thing, though. If I can do it anonymously, that's fine, but I won't put my name on anything. I don't want to be known as the town tattletale."

Sage nodded. "Good for you, Blossom. That's a great first step."

Chapter Twenty-Two

Two weeks later, she went to Kingston to pick up her car. It was a Wednesday; Cayenne's reception dinner and the wedding would be that weekend. They were wrapping up the first leg of the St. Ann project and a few of the workers returned to Kingston with them. They had a lively discussion about their favorite landscape designs.

When Bruce dropped her at the dealer, she forgot her camera and equipment in his vehicle, only remembering when Cayenne demanded to see their progress.

"Ah shucks," Sage said lazily. "I left my stuff in Bruce's vehicle."

"And there I was thinking I was going to get a sneak peek into the latest episode," Cayenne chuckled.

"I had no idea you would be so interested," Sage said.

"I wasn't that interested until the whole drama involving Aubry House." Cayenne shrugged. "It's exciting."

Sage called Bruce to tell him about the error. "I need to do some editing tonight," she said. "I might as well get some work done."

"Can you come over for it?" Bruce said tiredly. "I was about to have dinner. You are cordially invited to share it with me. Besides, I have not shown you around my section of the Kingston house. I know you are familiar with Brian's."

Anticipation zinged through Sage when she hung up the phone. "I am going over to Bruce's place for dinner."

Cayenne nodded. "Okay."

"I don't think he has seen me in a dress," Sage said as she got up. "My steady uniform over the past couple of weeks has been shorts, pants, casual wear. I am going to dress in something a bit more feminine."

Cayenne chuckled.

"And let out my hair and do a full face make-up."

"It's too obvious," Cayenne said. "Besides, he'll see you all dolled up this weekend."

"True," Sage squealed and ran upstairs.

Cayenne laughed.

Sage showered in record time, spritzed on her favorite perfume, and twirled in the mirror in her summer dress, which showed off a hint of sun-kissed cleavage and a good part of her legs.

Cayenne whistled when she sauntered downstairs. "You look awesome!"

"Thanks, sis." Sage grinned. "Wish me luck!"

"Good luck!" Cayenne called after her as Sage headed out the door, excitement bubbling within her.

Her excitement was short-lived. She knew where the house was; she had been to Brian's section countless times before. The house was a split-level building. The downstairs, where Brian lived, had been a cozy two-bedroom apartment with a small but functional kitchen, a comfortable living room, and a quaint dining area. She could already picture the familiar surroundings as she approached the house.

Upstairs, though, was another story. For starters, there was an intercom at the gate, and Bruce had transformed the gardens into a showpiece. Lush, well-tended flower beds lined the walkway, and neatly trimmed hedges framed the path. The sweet scent of blooming flowers wafted through the air, adding a touch of elegance to the already charming setting.

Sage pressed the intercom button and waited. Moments later, Bruce's voice crackled through the speaker. "Sage, is that you? Come on in." The gate opened, and she drove up the driveway, admiring the garden as she went.

She stepped onto the porch, intending to knock, when the door was yanked open.

"Surprise!" Brian said. "I just arrived after a long flight, and can you imagine when I got here, my dad was expecting you for dinner!"

Sage gasped. "Brian, you are a sight for sore eyes."

Brian scowled.

"Let her in, Brian," Bruce said from somewhere behind him. "She is my guest."

Brian stepped aside and made a sweeping gesture with his hand. "Yes, sir."

Sage barely squeezed past him. He was glaring at her intensely.

"What has you so mad?" Sage whispered.

"You, this situation, my dad. Mostly you." Brian ran his hand through his hair. He needed a trim; his curls were overly long.

He still looked good, though. Her eyes skittered from his handsome face to the interior of the house. It looked amazing with its high ceilings, large windows, and tasteful décor.

"Welcome, Sage," Bruce said easily. "I held dinner until you got here. Brian said he would join us."

Brian grunted. "Why are you so dressed up and looking so pretty?"

"I, er," Sage looked down at her dress, "this old thing."

"I'll give you a tour when we are done eating, Sage," Bruce said, rescuing her from the awkward face-off with Brian. "But the food is getting cold."

Bruce led her through a spacious living room adorned with art pieces and comfortable furniture. They passed a modern kitchen that gleamed with stainless steel appliances and marble countertops before arriving at the dining area, where a beautifully set table awaited them.

The tension was so thick you could cut it with a knife.

Bruce sat at the head of the table; she sat to his right, and Brian to his left.

"Well," Bruce said, "it's a good thing I ordered more than enough food, isn't it?"

Sage nodded.

Brian scowled.

Brian kept glancing between her and Bruce. "It's my dad, isn't it? This new relationship? The one you wanted me to be cool about?"

"Brian," Bruce said, "can we eat and talk after?"

"No," Brian said sullenly. "I can't eat when my girlfriend could be my stepmother."

"I am not your girlfriend," Sage said. "We broke up. I was begging for you to end it with me."

"So that you could date my father!" Brian yelled. "I do not want you to date my father. It's weird! And icky!"

"Brian, please," Bruce interjected. "This is childish."

Brian laughed dryly. "Heard that, Sage? My dad thinks we are acting childish."

"Okay," Bruce said. "Brian quit this. You are acting immature. She broke up with you; move on."

"You should fire her, Dad," Brian said.

"I'm not going to fire Sage," Bruce said. "You will have to find a way to be cordial around her."

"It's never going to happen," Brian said. "As long as you two are together in whatever capacity, I am done."

"No, it's fine," Sage said. "I'll quit after this. I don't want to be a source of contention in your relationship."

"Come on, Sage," Bruce said. "You love your job, and you're great at it. I'm not letting you walk away because of this."

Sage pushed away from the table. "I am sorry, I can't eat with the hostility. Let's face it, I always knew this would happen. I don't want to be the person who comes between you and your son. Where are my things?"

"I left them in the hallway," Bruce said. He pushed away from the table. "I'll get them for you."

"No, I'll get it," Sage said.

"Sage, wait," Bruce said earnestly. "You can't just leave at the first sign of adversity."

"That's how young people are," Brian said smugly, "fickle and feckless."

Sage saw her gear, grabbed it up with tears in her eyes, and headed through the front door.

Chapter Twenty-Three

"She left you so easily; she offered to quit almost immediately," Brian said when Sage left and started calmly eating. "Aren't you happy I saved you from her?"

Bruce shook his head. "She was distressed. Your performance was reprehensible. I told you not to do this. You said you would be the picture of civility. Is this civility?"

"I couldn't help myself," Brian shrugged. "I had to punish her a little for moving on with you. I know she had a crush on you. It was all over for us from the moment she met you. I resented it, but what could I do? I expected it to pass. I didn't know you would reciprocate. You like older women. Sage is so not your type."

"I know," Bruce said, "but I love her."

"I can't believe Sage might end up being my stepmother," Brian chuckled. "We will have very interesting family dinners from now on. When you told me that you were dating her two weeks ago, I was a little distraught at first, but then

I started seeing the humor in the whole thing. I might have been devastated if she and I had been intimate, but lucky for you, old man, we didn't go far. A peck here and there on the lips is all we've done. Sage is not one to jump into intimacy."

"I know," Bruce said. "I like that about her."

"So, what now?" Brian asked.

"You will apologize for this evening," Bruce said. "Tell her you were being dramatic to wind her up. I booked an Airbnb in St. Mary, where the wedding will be this weekend. I will make up with her then."

"Yes, I'll apologize when you guys return," Brian nodded. "I have plans this weekend too. I'll be going over to St. Ann. Natalia is expecting me."

"You two finally figured things out, huh?" Bruce said.

"Yes," Brian nodded. "I can't believe she had me jealous over Shane all this time. I literally started grinding my teeth in my sleep. I was so distressed. She almost made me fail my exams."

Bruce frowned. "It bothers me that you were so into Natalia while you were with Sage."

"I know," Brian said. "I was like a dog in a manger. And that's one more thing I must apologize to Sage for."

"Good." Bruce nodded.

"I guess you can't help who you love, huh, Dad? I thought I was over Natalia when I started dating Sage, but I just couldn't shake her out of my mind and heart. I think I am going to end up loving her forever."

Bruce smiled. "I am happy things are working out for you, Brian."

****

"You are going to look haggard for the pictures," Anise said fretfully, peering into Sage's face when they arrived at

Sea Glass Villa. "The reception dinner is in a few hours. Did you have to stay up all night and edit the video for Bruce? Doesn't he know you have an important role in your sister's wedding?"

"I had to do it. I couldn't sleep anyway," Sage said despondently, sprawling out on the bed. It was a packed house so she was sharing a room with Anise. "I was thinking about yesterday and dinner. And how I told him I would quit, and Brian's snarling face saying he didn't want me to date his father. I didn't want Bruce to choose."

"I will speak with that spoiled brat Brian when I get back from the wedding," Anise said. "He made you sad."

"Ah, Mom, don't get involved," Sage said. "I'll hand in my resignation to Bruce on Monday and label this part of my life as my delusional stage. I fell in love with my boyfriend's father; what did I expect, a happy ending?"

"Well, why not?" Anise said. "I can't believe Bruce would just let you go like that. I was looking forward to hearing what Grandma Saidie says about him."

"She'd like him," Sage said, putting a pillow over her face. "He is one of the good ones, a decent man."

"If he doesn't show up tonight, he didn't deserve you anyway," Anise huffed. "Now you are making me upset on your behalf."

"Don't be; it's a happy occasion," Sage said. "I am going to take a nap and get up with my game face on."

Chapter Twenty-Four

It was a perfect night for a reception dinner by the sea. The gentle breeze carried the scent of saltwater and mingled with the delicate aroma of the flowers adorning the tables. Strings of fairy lights twinkled on poles leading to the beach. The waves lapping against the shore provided a soothing backdrop to the laughter and clinking of glasses.

The festivities hadn't begun yet. A lone saxophonist was playing, and people were still trickling in. Sage stood with her back to all the activity, closer to the pier in the half-dark. She figured she looked like a lonely figure in her floaty white dress.

She felt bereft. She finally understood what it was to be lonely in a crowd. It was just sinking in that she had offered to quit her job and her new relationship with Bruce just because Brian said he didn't want her to be with his father.

Who was he to tell her that? And why didn't Bruce say something? He didn't love her enough, that's why. And he probably secretly wanted her to quit anyway. She was the one pushing for a relationship; he had never been comfortable with her age.

Sage heard his voice near her ears. She shuddered. Why was she imagining him? Then she felt his hand on her shoulder.

"I hope I am not too late, but I see the party hasn't started yet."

"Bruce!" She spun around and looked into his handsome face. He was cleanly shaven, dressed in black jeans and a white shirt that fit him like a glove. "You came," she said.

"Of course I did," Bruce said. "We left things unresolved yesterday."

"But Brian said…"

"He will call and apologize and tell you he was being dramatic. I told him two weeks ago about us. He did all his ranting and raving then. He went through all the stages of grief with me and finally acceptance. Of course, the fact that Natalia is free and not going to marry Shane had a lot to do with his sanguine approach. Yesterday was just an act; you left before he could tell you."

"Oh." Sage opened her mouth. "I was devastated. It was my nightmare coming true. I knew you would choose Brian over me."

"Shhh." Bruce placed a finger over her lips. "I will say this many times in the future, and I am saying it now. I'll always choose you."

Sage inhaled. "So you're fine now with our age gap?"

Bruce smiled, his eyes softening. "I care more about you than our age difference. And I've realized that nothing else matters to me but you and your happiness."

Sage felt tears well up in her eyes. "I've been so worried, so afraid that we'd never get past this."

He took her hands in his, squeezing them gently. "We will. We'll face everything together. I promise."

She nodded, feeling a weight lift off her shoulders. "Thank you, Bruce. For coming tonight, for choosing me."

He leaned in, pressing his forehead against hers. "Always. Let's put all this behind us and focus on our future."

Sage smiled, her heart swelling with hope. "Yes, let's do that. But first, I will have to introduce you to Grandma Saidie."

Bruce pulled her into a tight embrace, and she felt safe and secure in his arms. They stood there for a moment, wrapped up in each other, ready to face whatever came next, together.

Epilogue

One year later

It was a garden wedding at Aubry House. Sage was dressed in a simple white sheath dress. She had opted not to have a bridal party. Cayenne was heavily pregnant and not up to being a bridesmaid. Cinnamon would be her matron of honor, and Brian would be Bruce's best man. It worked into her vision for her wedding anyway: a simple garden wedding with just their closest family and friends.

The three sisters and Anise were sitting in the library suite before the ceremony, which would be held on the terrace. It was a clear day, quite cool and windy. Sage was ensuring that her flower headband was fastened tightly to her curly updo. She didn't want it to blow off while walking down the aisle.

"You look so happy," Cayenne said, blinking back tears. "I mean, it is literally radiating off you."

Cinnamon nodded. "I know, right? Sage is glowing. So why are you crying?"

"Pregnancy hormones," Cayenne said. "Even happiness makes me cry."

Cinnamon chuckled. "Dirk said you've been crying every day. I guess that means you are really happy."

"I am," Cayenne sniffed. "I've only been focusing on positive things. I want a peaceful, zen pregnancy for Saffron Diamond."

Sage chuckled. "I will buck the trend when I have a baby and call her something completely unrelated to a spice and stone."

Cinnamon chuckled. "No, you won't. You'll bow to pressure just like I did. And didn't I hear Bruce saying it is only fitting that his business is landscaping, and he is marrying a flower? Trust and believe that man will follow our family's naming trend."

"True," Sage giggled.

"Well, I am quite happy with whatever trend you want to start in your own family," Anise said, pouring some wine.

"I can't have wine," Cayenne said.

"Oh, this is non-alcoholic," Anise said. "It's from our newest line of non-alcoholic wines. This is a limited edition, done in consultation with one Mr. Bruce Whitlock."

"It's purple," Sage looked over her shoulder.

"It is," Anise smiled. "The color of amethyst, with a hint of sage, pineapple, mango, and ginger. It's quite the unique blend, just like you, Sage."

"And the name of it is..." Cinnamon looked at the bottle. "Sage Amethyst, named after the bride."

Sage smiled, taking a sip from the glass Anise had handed her. "Thanks, Mom. It's delicious and fruity, and the color is perfect."

"I want to propose a toast to my girls." Anise said, "I may not have had any of you under the best circumstances, but I wouldn't trade any of it for the world. You three are my greatest accomplishments and my endless source of joy. To Sage, on this your special day, and to Cayenne and Cinnamon, for always being there for each other. Cheers to love, family, and new beginnings."

They all raised their glasses, the purple liquid shimmering in the light. "Cheers!" they echoed, clinking their glasses together.

Sage felt warmth spread through her as she sipped the drink. The flavors melded perfectly, and she could taste the subtle hint of ginger at the end. It was a perfect reflection of the love and effort her family put into everything.

There was another knock at the door; this time, it was Horace, looking a bit teary-eyed. "Ladies, it's time."

Sage took a deep breath and stood, her heart pounding with a mix of excitement and nerves. She hugged her sisters and mother before stepping into the hallway with Horace.

As they walked towards the terrace, Sage felt a sense of calm wash over her. The garden was in full bloom, the colors vibrant, and the air filled with the sweet scent of flowers.

When they reached the terrace, Sage saw Bruce standing at the altar, his eyes fixed on her. He looked incredibly handsome in his tailored suit, the amethyst boutonnière standing against the dark fabric. His smile was warm and reassuring, and it gave Sage the confidence she needed.

Horace squeezed her hand and whispered, "You look beautiful, honey. I am honored to be a part of this important day."

"Thank you, Horace," Sage replied, her voice filled with emotion.

As they walked down the aisle together, Sage felt the love

and support of everyone around her. She caught glimpses of smiling faces, friends, and family all gathered to witness this special moment.

When they reached the altar, Horace kissed Sage on the cheek and handed her over to Bruce. The officiant began the ceremony, his voice carrying over the gentle breeze.

Sage and Bruce exchanged vows, their words filled with love and promise. As they slipped the rings onto each other's fingers, Sage felt a sense of completeness she had never known before.

"You may now kiss the bride," the officiant declared.

Bruce cupped her face gently in his hands and kissed her, the applause and cheers of their guests filling the air.

The reception that followed was a joyous celebration. The Sage Amethyst wine was a hit, with guests marveling at its unique flavor. Cayenne, Cinnamon, and Anise each took turns dancing with Sage, their laughter and love lighting up the night.

As the evening drew to a close, Sage and Bruce stood together under the stars, holding hands and looking out over the garden. The lights twinkled around them, and the soft hum of conversation and music filled the air.

"I love you, Bruce," Sage whispered, resting her head on his shoulder.

"I love you too, Sage," Bruce replied, kissing the top of her head. "Here's to our forever."

Dear Reader,

THANK YOU for reading Sage, the final book in the Spice and Stone series. I hope you enjoyed the book and the stories of these three women. I initially intended to write just Cinnamon. It was supposed to be a stand-alone title, and then I would move on to the next project. However, Cayenne and Sage had their stories to be told, and I just had to tell them.

Speaking of my next project, it's a five-book series inspired by characters from the Crimson Hill series, particularly those in No Place Like You (Crimson Hill Series Book 8). Jewel's friends, Camden, Kenny, and Audra, will get their own books, and other characters from that series, like DJ Duke and Richard Tinsdale, will also be a part of that series. You'll even see Anise again in this series because I believe she deserves a happy ending like her daughters.

I am looking forward to bringing you The Ridgeview Series. Continue reading for an excerpt from Book 1, Ride or Die.

Warmest Regards,

Brenda

Excerpt Ride or Die (Ridgeview Book 1)

Two Years Ago

It was a double celebration: Camden Byfield's twenty-seventh birthday and housewarming party. The night was perfect; it had rained earlier, and the place was significantly cooler now. A gentle wind was blowing, and she could smell the white roses that were planted in giant pots on the opposite sides of the patio.

Kenny had excused herself from the joyous occasion inside to take a breather. It wasn't that it was a bad party or even dull. It was her—she felt off, maybe a little sad. What was wrong with her? She should be happy for Camden's successes; this house purchase was a huge deal for him. It was one more step toward "adulting," as he had called it. And she was the one who had set things in motion.

She had casually suggested that Camden buy into the Ridgeview townhouse complex after hearing about it from Richard Tinsdale, one of her clients who was a property developer. When Richard decided to dip his toes into the luxury market, he summoned her and Jewel, his app developers, to his office. "I want some changes to the app," he had told them. "I am going luxury."

It was Richard's first high-end development of six townhouses on a bluff overlooking the sea. He had toyed with several names but eventually settled on Ridgeview.

For the past year, she and Camden had a long-standing date at Freddy's Pier, where they would sit, chat, and unburden on each other about the week. They were the only singles in their friendship group in Jamaica.

Kent and Moses, the IT company where she worked, was

just a stone's throw away from Byfield and Byfield, the law firm where Camden was a lawyer.

She had told Camden about the development, and he had shown interest. For a few years, he had expressed an interest in leaving his parents' guest house and venturing out on his own.

"It's high time, Kenny," he had said, looking at her without his characteristic grin. "I'm ready to make big moves, turn my own key, be the man of my house. Start adulting."

Kenny had laughed.

Camden did not. "I'm not joking, Kenny."

"If you're serious, you should call Richard. He said people are interested in the place even before the houses are finished."

"Tell me more about them," Camden had nodded.

"Three bedrooms, three and a half baths, a large land space, and the view is said to be superb," Kenny said. "Richard used the words 'premium' and 'luxury.' I haven't seen them to ascertain what that looks like, but he had us designing a home app for opening the front door remotely and many other cool features."

"Is there yard space for kids to play?" Camden asked.

Kenny had looked at Camden, shocked. "Why?"

"Because I may want a kid or two," Camden said. "I like Rory and Jewel's kid; he's cute and smart."

"That's a given," Kenny said. "Look at his parents. Jewel was reading Algorithms To Live By while she was pregnant with him. She even gave him Isaac Newton's first name."

Camden nodded. "It got me thinking—most of our friends are parents. Maybe I should be looking in that direction. I want a smart kid, too."

"It doesn't work like that," Kenny chuckled. "Besides, don't you need a serious relationship for that to happen? And you're not going to commit until you're forty, remember? You're not even seeing anyone now."

"True, but I have someone in mind," Camden had said mysteriously. "To be honest with you, I've always had her in mind. I wanted to get the wildness out of my system first. I think I'm at the stage where I can present myself to her and say, 'Hey, I'm serious and ready to be the mature, non-goofy person you've always wanted me to be.'"

Kenny shook her head. "I can't imagine you being non-goofy. Which girl would want that? You're handsome, but your personality is what's most attractive about you. There is never a dull day with you around."

"Okay, then, I'll be my same old goofy self around her," Camden smiled. "But I'll never be goofy about my feelings."

That was eight months ago; she had never asked him who the mystery girl was because she didn't want to seem too interested in his love life. As close as they were, they never really spoke about his various relationships. He was certainly interested in hers, but she usually didn't have much to report. She had one serious relationship, but they broke up around the same time she and Camden started hanging out on the weekends. She hadn't been heartbroken; Camden had made sure of that.

She looked at him now through the patio doors, holding court in his tastefully furnished luxurious home, laughing at a joke and being his adorable, handsome self. For a moment, she slipped. She wished she was by his side, with her hand around his neck, her body pressed to his side, entertaining their guests together.

She turned her back to Camden and looked out at the view. The sea was supposed to be uninteresting at night, but the moon cast a silvery glow over the water, turning it into a shimmering, black glass with sparkles.

She was slipping a lot lately. Camden was her friend, her bestie, her ride-or-die. They had known each other since prep school. In fact, he had been her first crush. For a brief time in high school, they had even considered themselves in a relationship, which had fizzled out almost as soon as it began. They had quarreled about Camden liking the new girl in their third-form class a bit too much.

"I can't be tied down now," Camden had told her in no uncertain terms. "There are so many pretty girls in this school to have relationships with, not just you. I think that having a girlfriend every week would be a perfect solution to my problem."

Kenny had kicked him on the shin and slapped him on the head with her Geography textbook because of that breakup speech.

He had howled with anger. "That's it! We are done! We are no longer boyfriend and girlfriend or even ordinary friends. We will not even talk to each other again!"

Kenny had stomped on his foot for good measure. She knew it would hurt; he had football practice later that evening and she wanted him to suffer.

But when she saw that he had left his water bottle in the classroom after their last class, she had taken it to him at practice.

He had approached her cautiously and taken the bottle from her. "About earlier today, I take it back."

"What are you taking back?" Kenny snarled.

"I'll always be your friend," Camden grinned. "I solemnly swear."

"Save it," Kenny had growled. "You're thirteen years old; you can't solemnly swear anything."

"But I do," Camden corrected her. "And you'll have to swear, too. Solemnly swear that you'll be my friend forever."

"I won't," Kenny had grimaced. "We won't even speak to each other after high school. I'll pass you in the streets in my luxury vehicle and deliberately drive in a puddle so that I can splash you from head to toe."

Camden laughed. "Kenny, you won't always be mad at me. One day, you'll forget all this, and then we'll be friends again. And tell you what, when we are old, we'll try the boyfriend and girlfriend thing again."

"How old are we talking?" Kenny frowned.

"Twenty-six, that seems ancient enough," Camden said. "Give me thirteen more years."

"By twenty-six, I'll be married and have at least two children," Kenny had snickered. "So sorry you'll miss out on all of this." She indicated her body.

Camden laughed and ran back to his game.

Kenny sighed, her trip down memory lane had only highlighted that next month, November, would be her twenty-seventh birthday. She had been so wrong then about her future, but Camden seemed on track with his—except it was not with her. There was the mystery woman—the one who had always been on his mind, the one he was finally ready to pursue. It made her stomach tighten, a feeling she didn't understand and didn't want to explore too deeply. Why was she so reluctant to hear who it was, she didn't know.

Camden was her closest friend at the moment; they told each other everything. He was even closer to her than her girlfriends, Jewel and Audra. Jewel was busy with her young family and rarely had time to do girly stuff these days, and Audra was pursuing her residency at medical school in the States. She only returned to Jamaica for brief visits, and usually, she had her son with her. They couldn't talk about adult stuff with an inquisitive four-year-old around.

Kenny inhaled deeply. She was leaving for her lonely

apartment and her confused feelings and convoluted thoughts about Camden.

She spun around just as Camden was coming onto the patio.

"Kenny, I wondered where you had disappeared to."

"I didn't know you would have noticed I was gone," Kenny said hoarsely. She cleared her throat.

"But of course, I always notice where you are in a room," Camden said ruefully. "It's a habit of mine."

"I was thinking of going home."

"It's early," Camden said, walking closer to her. "And I wanted to say something to you after everyone leaves."

"I'm not staying behind to help you clean up," Kenny frowned.

Camden chuckled. "I have a housekeeping service for that. I scheduled them to come by at seven tomorrow."

"Oh, well then," Kenny inhaled. "Can we talk tomorrow?"

"Nope," Camden said. "Stay right there. Give me ten minutes, and I'll end this party."

Kenny nodded. "Okay."

It took him closer to twenty minutes.

Kenny had stretched out on the lounger and closed her eyes when she felt him beside her.

"Scoot over," Camden said.

She moved over, and he sank down beside her.

"You smell so good," Kenny inhaled. "Has anybody ever told you that you wear the best colognes?"

Camden chuckled. "I hear that all the time, thanks to you. You buy my colognes."

"So, what do you want to talk about?" Kenny asked.

"Do you ever think about the future?" Camden asked, his tone unusually serious.

Kenny nodded. Their faces were close to each other.

"Sometimes. I mean, who doesn't?"

"I'm not talking about just any future. I'm talking about... our future."

"Our future?" Kenny's heart skipped a beat. What was he getting at?

Camden caressed her cheek. "We've been friends for so long, and I've been thinking... maybe it's time we tried something more."

The words hung in the air, heavy and unexpected. Kenny stared at him, her mind racing. Was she his mystery girl?

"I can't keep pretending I don't feel something more for you than friendship," Camden whispered. "I've been falling for you for a long time, and I'm ready to see where this could go."

Kenny looked into his eyes, searching for any hint of the old Camden she knew—the one who always had a joke ready and was never serious about anything except his work. But all she saw was sincerity. And maybe, just maybe, that was what scared her the most.

"I don't know what to say," she whispered. "I thought you were going to tell me about your mystery girl."

"The mystery girl is you," Camden said. "I've been giving you broad hints about my changing feelings and intentions for months, but you've ignored them."

"But..." Kenny whispered.

"We've been hanging out for the past year, spending every moment together," Camden said. "I hated going home without you after our Friday night dates. I think you should move in with me."

"Move in?" Kenny chuckled. "We've never even kissed."

Camden pulled her toward him and placed his lips on hers.

Kenny froze momentarily, her mind racing to catch up with the sudden shift in their relationship. But as Camden's lips moved gently against hers, all her doubts began to melt away. She felt a warmth spreading through her, a sense of rightness she hadn't expected. She leaned into the kiss, letting herself fall into the moment.

When they finally pulled apart, they were breathing heavily.

"Wow," Kenny murmured. "I had no idea you were such a good kisser."

"If you move in with me, we'll kiss every day. I'll get to be an even better kisser," Camden murmured.

"Okay," she whispered, her voice trembling slightly. "I'll do it. No, what am I saying? My mother will have a heart attack over this. There's no proposal here..."

"I'll propose," Camden said, "but only after we've lived together for two years. Then we'll assess the state of our relationship. Those are the terms; will you agree to them?"

Discover Exclusive Offers and Be the First to Know!

If you haven't already, don't miss out on the opportunity to join my New Release Newsletter! Sign up today and become part of an exclusive community where you'll be among the first to hear about my latest book releases and take advantage of special prices.

Why join my mailing list?

Be the First: Get a head start and be the first to know when I release a new book.

Exclusive Discounts: Unlock special prices available only to subscribers. Enjoy limited time offers and save big on your favorite books.

Quick and Easy: Signing up takes less than 30 seconds.

To join, visit https://www.brenalbar.com/newsletter or scan the QR code below.

Thank you for your support, and happy reading!

Ridgeview Series

The Ridgeview series follows five couples on the Jamaican north coast in the luxurious community of Ridgeview. It explores their everyday struggles with careers, children, and family drama. Each book touches on love, marriage, and trust as the characters face challenges that test their relationships.

Ride or Die (Book 1)
Play For Keeps (Book 2)
Through Thick and Thin (Book 3)
Tried and True (Book 4)
Stay With You (Book 5)

Spice and Stone Series

Join three extraordinary girls—Cinnamon, Cayenne, and Sage—as they navigate the intricate flavors of life, love, and romance in the captivating Spice and Stone series.

Cinnamon (Book 1)
Cayenne (Book 2)
Sage (Book3)

The Crimson Hill Series

Where family drama, romance, and a touch of sci-fi blend seamlessly in the enchanting backdrop of a small town in Jamaica. Prepare to embark on an unforgettable journey as secrets unravel, passions ignite, and destinies intertwine.

No Goodbye (Book 1)
No Misunderstanding (Book 2)
No Ordinary Love (Book 3)
No Fairy Tale (Book 4)
No Letting Go (Book 5)
No Strings Attached (Book 6)
No More Mrs. Nice Girl (Book 7)
No Place Like You (Book 8)
Knight and Day (Book 8.5)
No Expectations (Book 9)
Ice and Fyre (Book 9.5)
No Surrender (Book 10)
No Time for Love (Book 11)
No Promises (Book 12)
Winter's Eve (Book 13)

The Wiley Brothers

Step into the world of the Wiley Brothers, where tragedy weaves an unbreakable bond and love becomes their guiding light. In this captivating series, follow the journey of six remarkable boys as they navigate the tumultuous path of growing up without parents, discovering love, and finding their place in a challenging world.

Between Brothers (Book 0)- How it all began…
For Pete's Sake (Book 1)- Preston's story.
Crossing Jordan (Book 2)-Jordan's story.
Fire and Walter (Book 3)- Walter's story.
The Perfect Guy (Book 4)-Guy's Story.
The Patience of a Saint (Book 5)- Saint's Story.
A Case of Love (Book 6)- Case's Story.

The Pryce Sisters

Follow the remarkable journey of the Pryce triplets as they navigate the complexities of growing up, discovering romance, and embracing the exhilarating challenges of the new adult years.

Baby For A Pryce- Book 1
Right Pryce Wrong Time – Book 2
Yours, For A Pryce- Book 3

The Jacksons

Prepare to be enthralled by the captivating saga of the Jackson family. In this gripping series, secrets unravel, paternity questions loom, and love blooms in the most unexpected corners.

Ace- Book 1
Deuce- Book 2
Trey- Book 3
Quade- Book 4

The Scarlett Series

Their patriarch died and unexpectedly left each of them a fortune. Watch as the Scarlett family navigate their way through the ups and downs of sudden wealth, family secrets, and the complicated dynamics of their relationships.

Scarlett Baby (Book 1)
Scarlett Sinner (Book 2)
Scarlett Secret (Book 3)
Scarlett Love (Book 4)
Scarlett Promise (Book 5)
Scarlett Bride (Book 6)
Scarlett Heart (Book 7)

Magnolia Sisters

They were the rejects. The worst of the lot, they grew up in a girl's home together and formed sisterly bonds. Each book in the series tells the story of a different girl and the unique struggles and triumphs she faces along the way. With themes of friendship, forgiveness, and the power of love, the "Magnolia Sisters" series is a heartwarming and inspiring read that you won't want to put down.

Dear Mystery Guy- Book 1
Bad Girl Blues- Book 2
Her Mistaken Dream- Book 3
Just Like Yesterday – Book 4

New Song Series

A group of friends started out as a church band, see how each of them navigate their personal and professional lives while staying true to their faith and facing challenges along the way. With themes of forgiveness, redemption, and second chances, the New Song Series is a captivating read for anyone who enjoys heartwarming stories of love and faith.

Going Solo- Book 1
Duet on Fire- Book 2
Tangled Chords- Book 3
Broken Harmony- Book 4
A Past Refrain- Book 5
Perfect Melody- Book 6

The Bancrofts

The Bancroft family delves into the inner workings of academia and the high-stakes world of university politics. The family wrestles with the pressures of maintaining their family's legacy, they must confront their own demons and navigate the complex relationships that bind them together. From unexpected love affairs and betrayals to scandals and secrets that threaten to tear them apart, this is a series that will keep you captivated until the very end.

Homely Girl- Book 0
Saving Face- Book 1
Tattered Tiara- Book 2
Private Dancer- Book 3
Goodbye Lonely- Book 4
Practice Run- Book 5
Sense of Rumor- Book 6
A Younger Man- Book 7
Just To See Her- Book 8

Three Rivers Series

Three Rivers Series, a captivating tale of love, redemption, and second chances set in a picturesque community in St. Ann's Bay, Jamaica.

Private Sins- Book 1
Loving Mr. Wright- Book 2
Unholy Matrimony- Book 3
If It Ain't Broke- Book 4

The Resetter Series

The Resetter Series takes a look at a rare kind of person, a person who can travel back in time, but they only have one chance to get things right if they go back! With themes of second chances, changing the past and the power of love, the resetters series is a captivating time travel romance that many readers have described as a page turner.

Never Too Late- Book 1
Never Say Never- Book 2
Now or Never- Book 3
Almost Never- Book 4

On the Rebound Series

Experience the gripping and emotionally charged On the Rebound series, where love, betrayal, and redemption collide in a whirlwind of passion and secrets. Brace yourself for a journey filled with drama, cheating scandals, DNA questions, and ultimately, the power of second chances and finding love again.

On the Rebound- Book 1
On the Rebound Book 2

Standalone Books

Full Circle- After graduating from university, Diana wanted to return to Jamaica to find her siblings. What she didn't foresee was that she would meet Robert Cassidy and that both their pasts would be intertwined, and that disturbing questions would pop up about their parentage just when they were getting close.

After the End- Torn between two lovers. Colleen married her high school sweetheart, Isaiah, hoping that they would live happily ever after, but life intruded, and Isaiah disappeared at sea. She found work with the rich and handsome Enrique Lopez as a housekeeper and realized that she couldn't keep him at arm's length.

Love Triangle: Three Sides to the Story- George, the husband. Marie, the wife, and Karen-the mistress. They all get to tell their side of the story.

New Beginnings- Inner-city girl Geneva was offered an opportunity of a lifetime when she learned that her 'real' father was a wealthy man. Her decision to live up-town meant she had to leave Froggie, her 'ghetto don,' behind. She also found herself battling with her stepmother and battling her emotions for Justin, a suave up-towner.

The Preacher and the Prostitute- Prostitution and the clergy don't mix. Tell that to ex-prostitute Maribel, who finds herself in love with the Pastor at her church. Can an ex-prostitute and a pastor have a future together?

Historical Fiction

You won't want to miss out on these two captivating reads!

"The Pull of Freedom" tells the story of a slave family and their desperate struggle for freedom in Jamaica's colonial era. Follow the journey of these brave individuals as they fight for their right to be free, facing danger, heartbreak, and unimaginable obstacles along the way.

"The Empty Hammock" takes readers on a journey through time, as a modern woman finds herself transported back to the Taino era of Jamaica's history. Experience the wonder and mystery of this ancient culture through her eyes, as she learns about their traditions, beliefs, and way of life. With richly drawn characters and a beautifully realized setting, "The Empty Hammock" is a must-read for anyone who loves historical fiction that transports them to another time and place.

Short Story Collections

Di Taxi Ride and Other Stories- Funny stories about Jamaican life to make you laugh.

www.ingramcontent.com/pod-product-compliance
Lightning Source LLC
Chambersburg PA
CBHW051827150726

47998CB00001B/323